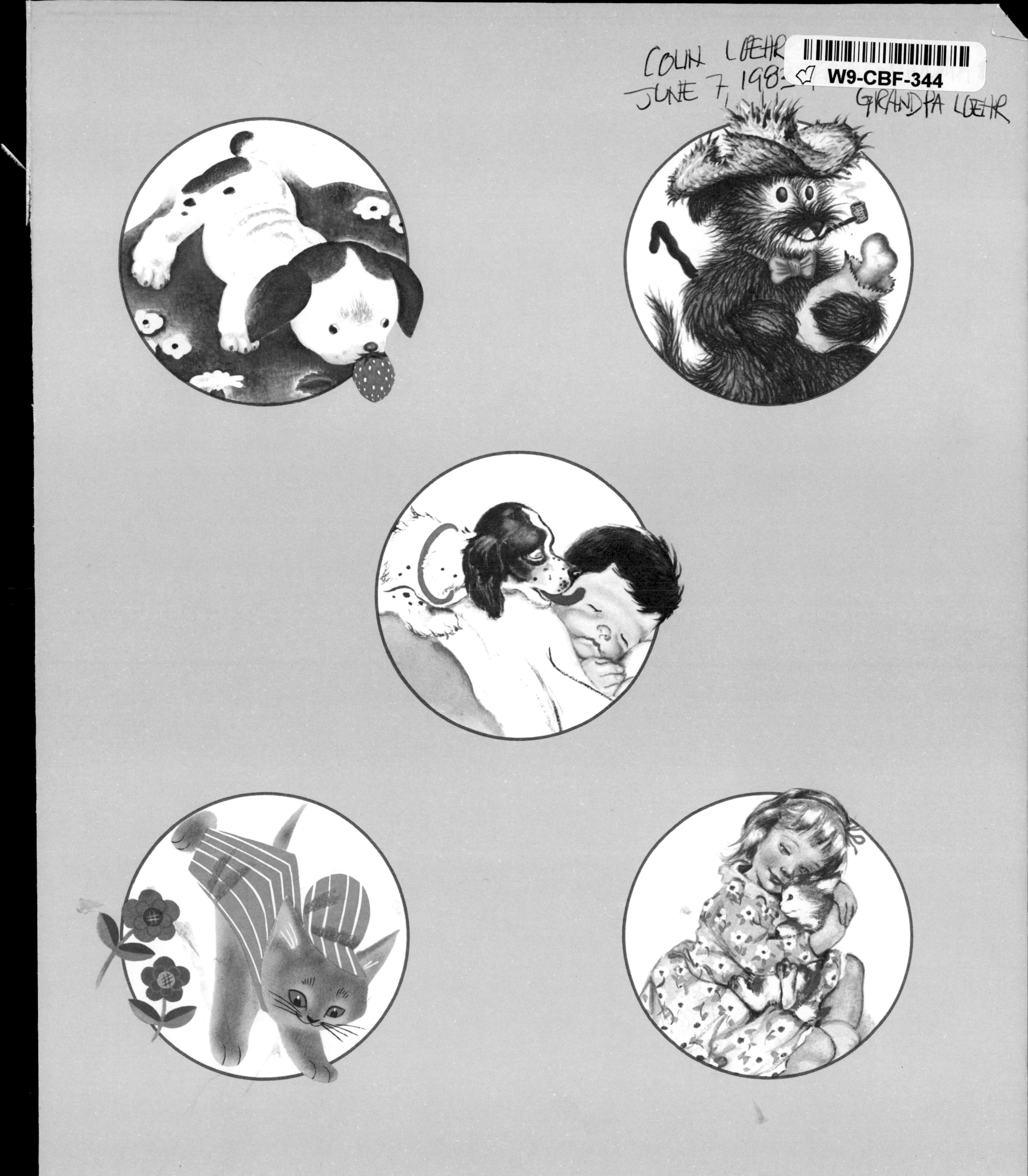

A Treasury of Little Golden Books

30 Best-Loved Stories

Selected and Edited by

ELLEN LEWIS BUELL

Revised and Abridged Edition

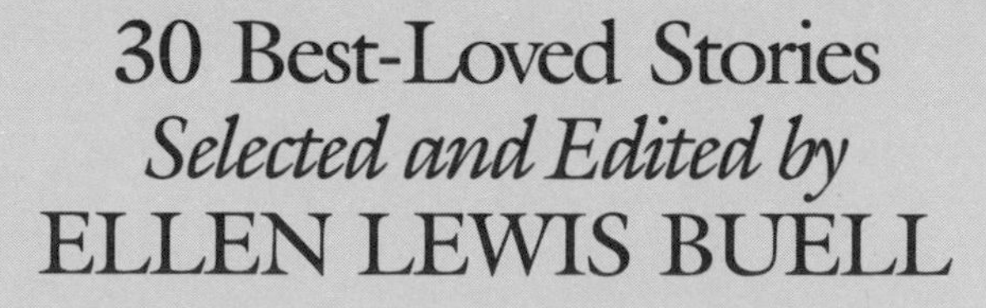

GOLDEN PRESS • NEW YORK
Western Publishing Company, Inc., Racine, Wisconsin

Cover art by Kathy Allert

 Library of Congress Catalog Card Number: 82-80361 ISBN 0-307-96540-6 A B C D E F G H I J

CONTENTS

THE POKY LITTLE PUPPY

by
JANETTE SEBRING LOWREY

illustrated by
GUSTAF TENGGREN

FIVE little puppies dug a hole under the fence and went for a walk in the wide, wide world.

Through the meadow they went, down the road, over the bridge, across the green grass, and up the hill, one after the other.

And when they got to the top of the hill, they counted themselves: one, two, three, four. One little puppy wasn't there.

"Now where in the world is that poky little puppy?" they wondered. For he certainly wasn't on top of the hill.

He wasn't going down the other side. The only thing they could see going down was a fuzzy caterpillar.

He wasn't coming up this side. The only thing they could see coming up was a quick green lizard.

But when they looked down at the grassy place near the bottom of the hill, there he was, running round and round, his nose to the ground.

"What is he doing?" the four little puppies asked one another. And down they went to see, roly-poly, pell-mell, tumble-bumble, till they came to the green grass; and there they stopped short.

"What in the world are you doing?" they asked.

"I smell something!" said the poky little puppy.

Then the four little puppies began to sniff, and they smelled it, too.

"Rice pudding!" they said.

And home they went, as fast as they could go, over the bridge, up the road, through the meadow, and under the fence. And there, sure enough, was dinner waiting for them, with rice pudding for dessert.

But their mother was greatly displeased. "So you're the little puppies who dig holes under fences!" she said. "No rice pudding tonight!" And she made them go straight to bed.

But the poky little puppy came home after everyone was sound asleep.

He ate up the rice pudding and crawled into bed as happy as a lark.

The next morning someone had filled the hole and put up a sign. The sign said:

BUT . . . . .

The five little puppies dug a hole under the fence, just the same, and went for a walk in the wide, wide world.

Through the meadow they went, down the road, over the bridge, across the green grass, and up the hill, two and two. And when they got to the top of the hill, they counted themselves: one, two, three, four. One little puppy wasn't there.

"Now where in the world is that poky little puppy?" they wondered. For he certainly wasn't on top of the hill.

He wasn't going down the other side. The only thing they could see going down was a big black spider.

He wasn't coming up this side. The only thing they could see coming up was a brown hop-toad.

But when they looked down at the grassy place near the bottom of the hill, there was the poky little puppy, sitting still as a stone, with his head on one side and his ears cocked up.

"What is he doing?" the four little puppies asked one another. And down they went to see, roly-poly, pell-mell, tumble-bumble, till they came to the green grass; and there they stopped short.

"What in the world are you doing?" they asked.

"I hear something!" said the poky little puppy.

The four little puppies listened, and they could hear it,

too. "Chocolate custard!" they cried. "Someone is spooning it into our bowls!"

And home they went as fast as they could go, over the bridge, up the road, through the meadow, and under the fence. And there, sure enough, was dinner waiting for them, with chocolate custard for dessert.

But their mother was greatly displeased. "So you're the little puppies who will dig holes under fences!" she said. "No chocolate custard tonight!" And she made them go straight to bed.

But the poky little puppy came home after everyone else was sound asleep, and he ate up all the chocolate custard and crawled into bed as happy as a lark.

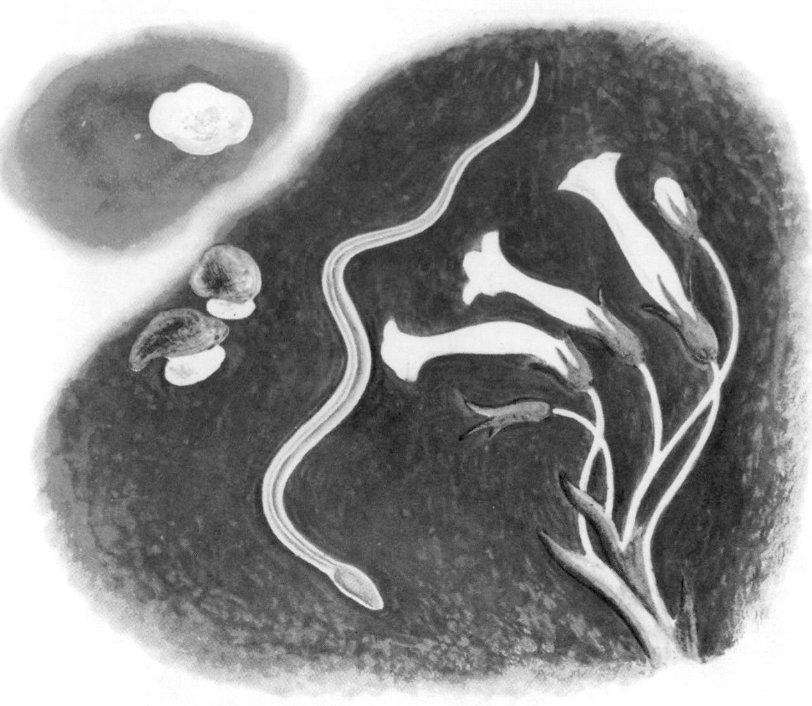

The next morning someone had filled the hole and put up a sign.

The sign said:

BUT . . . . .

In spite of that, the five little puppies dug a hole under the fence and went for a walk in the wide, wide world.

Through the meadow they went, down the road, over the bridge, across the green grass, and up the hill, two and two. And when they got to the top of the hill, they counted themselves: one, two, three, four. One little puppy wasn't there.

"Now where in the world is that poky little puppy?" they wondered. For he certainly wasn't on top of the hill.

He wasn't going down the other side. The only thing they could see going down was a little grass snake.

He wasn't coming up this side. The only thing they could see coming up was a big grasshopper.

But when they looked down at the grassy place near the bottom of the hill, there he was, looking hard at something on the ground in front of him.

"What is he doing?" the four little puppies asked one another. And down they went to see, roly-poly, pell-mell, tumble-bumble, till they came to the green grass; and there they stopped short.

"What in the world are you doing?" they asked.

"I see something!" said the poky little puppy.

The four little puppies looked, and they could see it, too. It was a ripe, red strawberry growing there in the grass.

"Strawberry shortcake!" they cried.

And home they went as fast as they could go, over the bridge, up the road, through the meadow, and under the fence. And there, sure enough, was dinner waiting for them, with strawberry shortcake for dessert.

But their mother said: "So you're the little puppies who dug that hole under the fence again! No strawberry shortcake for supper tonight!" And she made them go straight to bed.

But the four little puppies waited till they thought she was asleep, and then they slipped out and filled up the hole, and when they turned around, there was their mother watching them.

"What good little puppies!" she said. "Come have some strawberry shortcake!"

And this time, when the poky little puppy got home, he had to squeeze in through a wide place in the fence. And there were his four brothers and sisters, licking the last crumbs from their saucer.

"Dear me!" said his mother. "What a pity you're so poky! Now the strawberry shortcake is all gone!"

So poky little puppy had to go to bed without a single bite of shortcake, and he felt very sorry for himself.

And the next morning someone had put up a sign that read:

The ANIMALS *of* FARMER JONES

STORY BY LEAH GALE
PICTURES BY RICHARD SCARRY

IT IS supper time on the farm.
The animals are very hungry.
But where is Farmer Jones?

The horse stamps in his stall.
"I want my supper."
But where is Farmer Jones?

The sheep sniff around the barn.
"Ba-a-a, ba-a-a-a," say the sheep.
"We're waiting for supper.
But where is Farmer Jones?"

The cat rubs against a post.
"Me-o-w, me-o-w," says the cat.
"My dish is empty."
But where is Farmer Jones?

"Cluck, cluck," say the chickens.
"Give us our supper."
But where is Farmer Jones?

The ducks waddle out of the pond.
"Quack, quack," say the ducks.
"Supper time, supper time."
But where is Farmer Jones?

The pigs snuffle in the trough.
"Oink, oink," say the pigs.
"There's nothing to eat."
But where is Farmer Jones?

The cow jangles her bell.
"Moo, moo," says the cow.
"I am very hungry."
But where is Farmer Jones?

The dog runs about barking.
"Wuff, wuff," says the dog.
"I want my meal."
But where is Farmer Jones?

Farmer Jones is out in the field.
"Six o'clock!" says Farmer Jones.
"It's supper time!"
He goes to get food for the animals.

He gives oats to the horse.
"Nei-g-hh, nei-g-hh," says the horse.
"Thank you, Farmer Jones."

He gives turnips to the sheep.
"Ba-a-a, ba-a-a-a," say the sheep.
"Thank you, Farmer Jones."

He gives milk to the cat.
"Me-e-o-w, me-e-o-w," says the cat.
"Thank you, Farmer Jones."

He gives corn to the chickens.
"Cluck, cluck," say the chickens.
"Thank you, Farmer Jones."

He gives barley to the ducks.
"Quack, quack," say the ducks.
"Thank you, Farmer Jones."

He gives mash to the pigs.
"Oink, oink," say the pigs.
"Thank you, Farmer Jones."

He gives grain to the cow.
"Moo, moo," says the cow.
"Thank you, Farmer Jones."

He gives bones to the dog.
"Wuff, wuff," says the dog.
"Thank you, Farmer Jones."

"I am hungry, too," says Farmer Jones.
And off he goes for his supper.

TOOTLE

Story by
GERTRUDE CRAMPTON

Pictures by
TIBOR GERGELY

FAR, far to the west of everywhere is the village of Lower Trainswitch. All the baby locomotives go there to learn to be big locomotives. The young locomotives steam up and down the tracks, trying to call out the long, sad *ToooOooot* of the big locomotives. But the best they can do is a gay little *Tootle,* and the villagers smile as they listen to the young locomotives practice.

Lower Trainswitch has a fine school for engines. There are lessons in Whistle Blowing, Stopping for a Red Flag Waving, Puffing Loudly When Starting, Coming Around Curves Safely, Screeching When Stopping, Clicking and Clacking When Going Over the Rails, and Staying on the Rails No Matter What. Young locomotives must study all these lessons.

Then, too, there are other things to study. For those who wish to be freight trains there are How to Carry Milk Without Turning It to Butter, Freight Train Whistling, and Watching the Caboose. For passenger trains there are lessons in Going Through Tunnels, Pulling the Diner Without Spilling the Soup, and How Beds Are Made in Trains.

Of all the things that are taught in the Lower Trainswitch School for Locomotives, the most important is, of course, Staying on the Rails No Matter What.

The head of the school is an old engineer named Bill. Bill always tells the new locomotives that he will not be angry if they sometimes spill the soup pulling the diner, or if they turn the milk to butter now and then. But they will never, never be good trains unless they get 100 A+ in Staying on the Rails No Matter What. All the baby engines work very hard to get 100 A+ in Staying on the Rails. After a few weeks not one of the engines in the Lower Trainswitch School for Trains would even think of getting off the rails, no matter—well, no matter what.

One day a new locomotive named Tootle came to school.

"Here is the finest baby I've seen since old 600," thought Bill. He patted the gleaming young locomotive and said, "How would you like to grow up to be the Flyer between New York and Chicago?"

"If a Flyer goes very fast, I should like to be one," Tootle answered. "I love to go fast. Watch me."

He raced all around the roundhouse.

"Good! Good!" said Bill. "You must study Whistle Blowing, Puffing Loudly When Starting, Stopping for a Red Flag Waving, Pulling the Diner Without Spilling the Soup, and all kinds of things.

"But most of all you must study Staying on the Rails No Matter What. Remember, you can't be a Flyer unless you get 100 A+ in Staying on the Rails."

Tootle promised that he would remember and that he would work very hard. All the people in Lower Trainswitch began to talk about him. They said that he could pull a baby diner up hill and down again without spilling one drop of soup. And in just six lessons. They told about his high grades in Puffing, Whistle Blowing, and Clicking and Clacking. Tootle was the pet of the town.

He even worked hard at Stopping for a Red Flag Waving. Tootle did not like those lessons at all. There is nothing a locomotive hates more than stopping.

But Bill said that no locomotive *ever, ever* kept going when he saw a red flag waving.

"Stopping for a Red Flag Waving is almost as important as Staying on the Rails No Matter What," said Bill.

"Well, all right," Tootle grumbled. "I don't like to stop, though. I like to go fast."

"Yes, I know," said Bill. "You are like all Flyers. But you can go fast when you see the green flag."

One day, while Tootle was practicing for his lesson in Staying on the Rails No Matter What, a dreadful thing happened.

He looked across the meadow he was running through and saw a fine, strong black horse.

"Race you to the river," shouted the black horse, and kicked up his heels.

Away went the horse. His black tail streamed out behind him, and his mane tossed in the wind. Oh, how he could run!

"Here I go," said Tootle to himself.

"If I am going to be a Flyer, I can't let a horse beat me," he puffed. "Everyone at school will laugh at me."

His wheels turned so fast that they were silver streaks. The cars lurched and bumped together. And just as Tootle was sure he could win, the tracks made a great curve.

"Oh, whistle!" cried Tootle. "That horse will beat me now. He'll run straight while I take the Great Curve."

Then the Dreadful Thing happened. After all that Bill had said about Staying on the Rails No Matter What, Tootle jumped off the tracks and raced alongside the black horse!

The race ended in a tie. Both Tootle and the black horse were happy. Tootle was pleased because the horse hadn't won, and the horse was happy because he had never before been so close to beating a locomotive. They stood on the bank of the river and talked.

"It's nice out here in the meadow," Tootle said.

"Yes, but I thought you fellows had to stay on the rails," said the horse in a puzzled way.

"We do, but I didn't," Tootle explained.

"Oh," said the horse.

When Tootle got back to school, he said nothing about leaving the rails. But he thought about it that night in the roundhouse.

"Tomorrow I will work hard," decided Tootle. "I will not even think of leaving the rails, no matter what."

And he did work hard. He practiced tootling so much that the Mayor Himself ran up the hill, his green coattails flapping, and said that everyone in the village had a headache and would he please stop TOOTLING.

So Tootle was sent to practice Staying on the Rails No Matter What.

As he came to the Great Curve, Tootle looked across the meadow. It was full of buttercups.

"It's like a big yellow carpet. How I should like to play in them and hold one under my searchlight to see if I like butter!" thought Tootle. "But no, I am going to be a Flyer and I must practice Staying on the Rails No Matter What!"

Tootle clicked and clacked around the Great Curve. His wheels began to say over and over again, "Do you like butter? Do you?"

"I don't know," said Tootle crossly. "But I'm going to find out."

He stopped much faster than any good Flyer ever does, unless he is stopping for a Red Flag Waving. The sparks

shot from his wheels and the eight bowls of soup rolled around and around. He hopped off the tracks and bumped along the meadow to the yellow buttercups.

"What fun!" said Tootle.

And he danced around and around and held one of the buttercups under his searchlight. Then he ran to the river and peeked into the quiet water to see if he liked butter.

"I do like butter!" cried Tootle. "I do!"

At last the sun began to go down, and it was time to hurry to the roundhouse.

That evening while the Chief Oiler was playing checkers with old Bill, he said, "It's queer. It's very queer, but I found grass between Tootle's front wheels today."

"Hmm," said Bill. "There must be grass growing on the tracks."

"Not on our tracks," said the Day Watchman, who spent his days watching the tracks and his nights watching Bill and the Chief Oiler play checkers.

Bill's face was stern. "Tootle knows he must get 100 A+ in Staying on the Rails No Matter What, if he is going to be a Flyer."

Next day Tootle played all day in the meadow. He watched a green frog and he made a daisy chain. He found a rain barrel, and he said softly, "Toot!" "TOOT!" shouted the barrel. "Why, I sound like a Flyer already!" cried Tootle.

That night the First Assistant Oiler said he had found a daisy in Tootle's bell. The day after that, the Second Assistant Oiler said that he had found hollyhock flowers floating in Tootle's eight bowls of soup.

And then the Mayor Himself said that he had seen Tootle chasing butterflies in the meadow. The Mayor Himself said that Tootle had looked very silly, too.

Early one morning Bill had a long, long talk with the Mayor Himself.

When the Mayor Himself left the Lower Trainswitch School for Locomotives, he laughed all the way to the village.

"Bill's plan will surely put Tootle back on the track," he chuckled.

Bill ran from one store to the next, buying ten yards of this and twenty yards of that and all you have of the other. The Chief Oiler and the First, Second, and Third Assistant Oilers were hammering and sawing instead of oiling and polishing. And Tootle? Well, Tootle was in the meadow watching the butterflies flying and wishing he could dip and soar as they did.

That afternoon everyone in Lower Trainswitch crowded into the Office of the Mayor Himself. "Yes, yes!" they shouted when the Mayor Himself asked if they wanted to help Tootle. Then the Mayor Himself said, "Bill has a plan. If you do just as he says, I think we can teach young Tootle how to be a Flyer."

After that, Bill stood up and said things like this: "Now, you know that all locomotives. . . . Of course, every locomotive. . . . As I say, the thing is. . . . And if you will. . . ."

Then all the people laughed and promised to help. When they went home, each had a piece of ten yards of this and the twenty yards of that nailed to one of the sticks the Oilers had hammered and sawed all morning.

Not a store in Lower Trainswitch was open the next day and not a person was at home. By the time the sun came up, every villager was hiding in the meadow along the tracks. And each of them had a red flag. It had taken all the red goods in Lower Trainswitch, and hard work by the Oilers, but there was a red flag for everyone.

Soon Tootle came tootling happily down the tracks.

"Today I shall watch the bluebirds very carefully. Perhaps I can find out how they fly," he said to himself, and played a gay little song on his whistle.

When he came to the meadow, he hopped off the tracks and rolled along the grass. Just as he was thinking what a beautiful day it was, a red flag poked up from the grass and waved hard. Tootle stopped, for every locomotive knows he must stop for a Red Flag Waving.

"I'll go another way," said Tootle.

He turned to the left and up came another waving red flag, this time from the middle of the buttercups.

"Oh, whistle!" said Tootle, and stamped his cowcatcher hard. "Very well, I will go to the right and play toot-TOOT with the rain barrel."

When he went to the right, there was another red flag.

There were red flags waving from the buttercups, in the

daisies, under the trees, near the bluebirds' nest, and even one behind the rain barrel.

"Whenever I start, I have to stop. Why did I think this meadow was such a fine place? Why don't I ever see a green flag?"

Just as the tears were ready to slide out of his boiler, Tootle happened to look back over his coal car. On the tracks stood Bill, and in his hand was a big green flag. "Oh!" said Tootle.

He puffed up to Bill and stopped.

"This is the place for me," said Tootle. "There are nothing but red flags for locomotives that get off their tracks."

"Hurray!" shouted the people of Lower Trainswitch, and jumped up from their hiding places. "Hurray for Tootle the Flyer!"

Now Tootle is a famous Two-Miles-a-Minute Flyer. The young locomotives listen to his advice.

"Work hard," he tells them. "Always remember to Stop for a Red Flag Waving. But most of all, Stay on the Rails No Matter What."

THE SAGGY BAGGY ELEPHANT

BY K. & B. JACKSON • ILLUSTRATED BY TENGGREN

A HAPPY little elephant was dancing through the jungle. He thought he was dancing beautifully, one-two-three-kick. But whenever he went one-two-three, his big feet pounded so that they shook the whole jungle. And whenever he went kick, he kicked over a tree or a bush.

The little elephant danced along leaving wreckage behind him, until one day, he met a parrot.

"Why are you shaking the jungle all to pieces?" cried the parrot, who had never before seen an elephant. "What kind of animal are you, anyway?"

The little elephant said, "I don't know what kind of animal I am. I live all alone in the jungle. I dance and I kick—and I call myself Sooki. It's a good-sounding name, and it fits me, don't you think?"

"Maybe," answered the parrot, "but if it does it's the only thing that *does* fit you. Your ears are too big for you, and your nose is away too big for you. And your skin is *much,* MUCH too big for you. It's baggy and saggy. You should call yourself Saggy-Baggy!"

Sooki sighed. His pants *did* look pretty wrinkled.

"I'd be glad to improve myself," he said, "but I don't know how to go about it. What shall I do?"

"I can't tell you. I never saw anything like you in all my life!" replied the parrot.

The little elephant tried to smooth out his skin. He rubbed it with his trunk. That did no good.

He pulled up his pants legs—but they fell right back into dozens of wrinkles.

It was very disappointing, and the parrot's saucy laugh didn't help a bit.

Just then a tiger came walking along. He was a beautiful, sleek tiger. His skin fit him like a glove.

Sooki rushed up to him and said:

"Tiger, please tell me why your skin fits so well! The parrot says mine is all baggy and saggy, and I do want to make it fit me like yours fits you!"

The tiger didn't care a fig about Sooki's troubles, but he did feel flattered and important, and he did feel just a little mite hungry.

"My skin always did fit," said the tiger. "Maybe it's because I take a lot of exercise. But . . ." added the tiger, ". . . if you don't care for exercise, I shall be delighted to nibble a few of those extra pounds of skin off for you!"

"Oh no, thank you! No, thank you!" cried Sooki. "I love exercise! Just watch me!"

Sooki ran until he was well beyond reach.

Then he did somersaults and rolled on his back. He walked on his hind legs and he walked on his front legs.

When Sooki wandered down to the river to get a big drink of water, he met the parrot. The parrot laughed harder than ever.

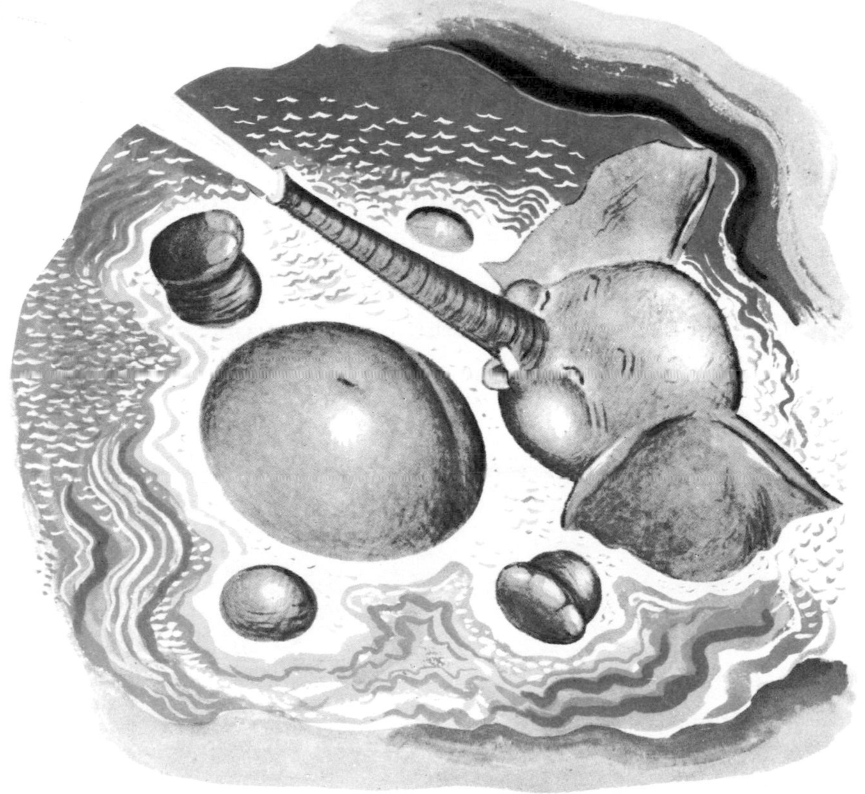

"I tried exercising," sighed the little elephant. "Now I don't know what to do."

"Soak in the water the way the crocodile does," laughed the parrot. "Maybe your skin will shrink."

So Sooki tramped straight into the water.

But before he had soaked nearly long enough to shrink his skin, a great big crocodile came swimming up, snapping his fierce jaws and looking greedily at Sooki's tender ears.

The little elephant clambered up the bank and ran away, feeling very discouraged.

"I'd better hide in a dark place where my bags and sags and creases and wrinkles won't show," he said.

By and by he found a deep dark cave, and with a heavy sigh he tramped inside and sat down.

Suddenly, he heard a fierce growling and grumbling and snarling. He peeped out of the cave and saw a lion padding down the path.

"I'm hungry!" roared the lion. "I haven't had a thing to eat today. Not a thing except a thin, bony antelope, and a puny monkey—and a buffalo, but such a tough one! And two turtles, but you can't count turtles. There's nothing much to eat between those saucers they wear for clothes! I'm *hungry!* I could eat an *elephant!*"

And he began to pad straight toward the dark cave where the little elephant was hidden.

"This is the end of me, sags, bags, wrinkles and creases," thought Sooki, and he let out one last, trumpeting bellow!

Just as he did, the jungle was filled with a terrible crashing and an awful stomping. A whole herd of great gray wrinkled elephants came charging up, and the big hungry lion jumped up in the air, turned around, and ran away as fast as he could go.

Sooki peeped out of the cave and all the big elephants smiled at him. Sooki thought they were the most beautiful creatures he had ever seen.

"I wish I looked just like you," he said.

"You do," grinned the big elephants. "You're a perfectly dandy little elephant!"

And that made Sooki so happy that he began to dance one-two-three-kick through the jungle, with all those big, brave, friendly elephants behind him. The saucy parrot watched them dance. But this time he didn't laugh, not even to himself.

The Taxi That Hurried

By LUCY SPRAGUE MITCHELL,
IRMA SIMONTON BLACK, AND JESSIE STANTON

Pictures by TIBOR GERGELY

ONCE there was a taxi. It was a bright yellow taxi with two red lines running around its body. Inside it had a soft leather seat and two hard little let-down seats.

It was a smart little taxi. For it could start fast—jerk-whizz!! It could tear along the street—whizz-squeak!! It could stop fast—squeak-jerk!!

Its driver's name was Bill. Together they were a speedy pair.

One day the taxi was standing on the street close to the sidewalk. Bill and the little taxi didn't like to stand still long. "I wonder who will be our next passengers," thought Bill.

Just then Bill heard some feet running on the sidewalk, thump, thump, thump! And he heard some smaller feet pattering along, too, thumpety, thumpety, thumpety!

He leaned out and saw Tom with a little suitcase and Tom's mother with a big suitcase. And both of them were breathing hard.

"Oh!" gasped Tom's mother. "Taxi driver-man, please drive us to the station as fast as you can. We're very late and the train won't wait. Oh!—oh!—oh!"

Tom and his mother tumbled into the taxi and slammed the door.

"Sure, lady," answered Bill. "We're a speedy pair. We can get you there."

Away went the taxi.

It liked to tear along in a hurry, purring softly. It rushed down the street like a yellow streak with the two red lines blurred into one around its middle. It wiggled through the traffic.

Tom and his mother bounced and jounced on the leather seats. Tom's mother sat on the wide, soft one behind. But Tom sat on a little hard one so that he could look out of the window.

Then suddenly, squeak-jerk! The taxi stopped short. It stood stock still in the middle of the street. Ahead shone a

bright red light. Underneath the light stood a big traffic policeman holding up his right hand.

Tom's mother called through the window, "Taxi driver-man, must you stop when lights are red? We simply have to get ahead. We're *terribly* late and the train won't wait."

And Bill answered, "Surely, lady, you have seen how cars must wait till lights are green. But we're a speedy pair, we'll surely get you there." Then suddenly, jerk-whizz! They were off again down the crowded street.

For the light had changed to green again.

Away went the taxi down the street faster than ever. Now it had to turn and twist, for the street was full of traffic—trucks and wagons and other taxis. The little taxi hurried past them all like a yellow streak and people could hardly see Tom's little face looking out of the window as he bounced and jounced by. "My!" said the people on the sidewalk. "That's a speedy taxi. I wonder why it's in such a hurry. Lucky it's got such a good driver." The taxi wiggled around a big bus. It jiggled across a trolley track. Then suddenly, squeak-jerk! The little taxi stopped short again.

It stood stock still behind a big coal truck that was backing up to the sidewalk. For the driver was trying hard to get his truck just the right way for the black coal to go jumping and clattering down its slide into a hole in the sidewalk.

Tom stood up so that he could see the big coal truck better. He could see the handle on the side. He wished he could watch the driver turn that handle and make the big truck tip up in front. He almost wished they weren't in a hurry.

Tom's mother called through the window: "Taxi driver-man, first it's a cop that makes you stop and now we're stuck behind a truck. We're *awfully* late and the train won't wait."

So Bill called to the truck driver, "Please, will you try to let me get by?"

And the truck driver grinned and stopped his truck. Carefully and slowly Bill squeezed by the big coal truck, close to the sidewalk.

Bill called over his shoulder, "We're a speedy pair. We'll get you there."

Now the taxi went so fast that people skipped up onto the sidewalk as it went by and everyone thought: "That's the speediest taxi I ever saw!" Then suddenly, squeak-jerk! The taxi stopped short and Tom almost fell through the front window.

Tom's mother bounced so hard on the wide leather seat that her head whacked the ceiling of the taxi. Her hat slid down over one ear. Her big suitcase fell over with a bang on the floor and Tom's little suitcase hopped off the seat.

Tom's mother pulled her hat on straight again. Then she looked at her watch. Then she looked out of the window at all the taxis and buses and trucks.

Once more she called to Bill on the front seat:

"Taxi driver-man, first it's a cop that makes you stop, then

you get stuck behind a truck. Now the traffic is in our way. We're likely to sit here the rest of the day. We're *horribly* late and the train won't wait!"

So Bill began to blow his horn. "Honk! honk!" shrieked the little taxi. "Honk! honk! HONK!!!

"We want to go. You make us slow! We're a speedy pair. We want to get there. Honk! *Honk!"*

HONK!!! HONK!!!

The nearer they came to the station, the more taxis and buses and trucks there were on the street.

Past them all the speedy taxi wiggled and jiggled, twisting and turning and curving and dodging. Tom jounced so hard on the little let-down seat that he could hardly see all the trucks and taxis and wagons and buses on the street.

Suddenly they stopped, and Bill blew the horn again. "Honk! *Honk!* HONK!"

Down the street, up above the station, they could see the big station clock. In five minutes the train would go. They really were very, terribly, awfully, horribly late, and they knew the train wouldn't wait.

Then suddenly, jerk, jerk! The traffic began to move. First a taxi, then a bus, then a truck, then more taxis, more buses, more trucks, till the whole line was moving. The speedy little taxi wiggled through the traffic. It dodged around a bus and it twisted around a truck and it whizzed past a taxi. Tom's mother kept looking at the big station clock. It said four minutes before the train went. Then three minutes. Then two minutes—and the little taxi drew up by the station.

Tom jumped out of the taxi while his mother gave Bill the money. She grabbed her big suitcase. Tom grabbed his little suitcase. And off they ran, thump, thump, thump, thumpety, thumpety, thumpety.

Bill looked after them and grinned at his yellow taxi. "Sure," he said. "We're a speedy pair—we got them there."

And it was true. The conductor was just ready to signal the engineer to start.

But he saw Tom and his mother come running down the platform and he waited for them. He took the big suitcase from Tom's mother, held the door open for her, and handed her the big suitcase. Tom stepped on the train after her, panting from his run and holding his little suitcase.

"All aboard!" called the conductor, waving his hand to the engineer.

Then the conductor swung onto the train just as it began to move. "You're a fast runner," he said to Tom. And to Tom's mother he said, "Lady, you just made it."

Tom was still breathing hard but he managed to gasp out, "We made it—because—we had such a speedy taxi—and speedy driver. You should have seen—that taxi hurry!"

The NEW BABY

By RUTH *and* HAROLD SHANE
Illustrated by ELOISE WILKIN

MIKE lived in a white house. There was a green lawn around the house, and lots of pretty flowers.

Mike was sweeping the garage. Daddy was mowing the lawn. Mummy was in the house cooking supper.

A big red truck stopped in front of the house. The delivery man took a large box from the truck. He was bringing it to Mike's house.

What could it be? It wasn't Christmas, so it couldn't be a Christmas present. It wasn't a lawn mower. Daddy had a lawn mower. It wasn't a new tricycle. Mike had a new red tricycle.

"Hello," Mike said to the delivery man.

"Hello, there," said the delivery man.

"Is that for us?" asked Mike.

"Yes," replied the delivery man. He rang the doorbell.

"What's in the box?" Mike asked.

"It's a bathinette."

Mike wondered what a bathinette could be.

Mummy came to the door. "Please bring the box right in," she said to the man.

The delivery man put the box by the window. Then he went back to the truck and drove away.

Mike looked at the big box. "What's a bathinette, Mummy?" he asked.

Daddy came in before Mummy had time to answer. "Aha!" he said. "Here's our new bathinette."

"What IS a bathinette?" asked Mike again.

"A bathinette is a baby's bathtub," Daddy told Mike. "It's for the new baby."

For a minute Mike did not say anything.

"Whose baby?" he asked at last.

"OUR baby," Daddy said. "After a while we're going to have a new, little one."

Mike couldn't believe it!

"A BABY!" he said excitedly. "What will it be like?"

"Will it be a little girl?"

"Will it be a boy?"

"When is it coming here?"

"Will it have red hair like Susie next door?"

"Hold on a minute!" laughed Daddy. "We don't know what it will look like or whether it will be a little boy or a little girl. We can only guess. It's a surprise!"

"When will the baby be here?" Mike asked.

Daddy told Mike that the baby would come quite soon.

Then Mummy said, "Time for supper!" before Mike could ask even one more question.

Mike ate a big supper and he had a cookie for dessert. And all the time he wondered what the baby would be like, and thought of the fun he could have with a baby brother or sister.

A few days later Mike had another surprise. Aunt Pat was coming. Daddy, Mummy, and Mike went to the station to meet her.

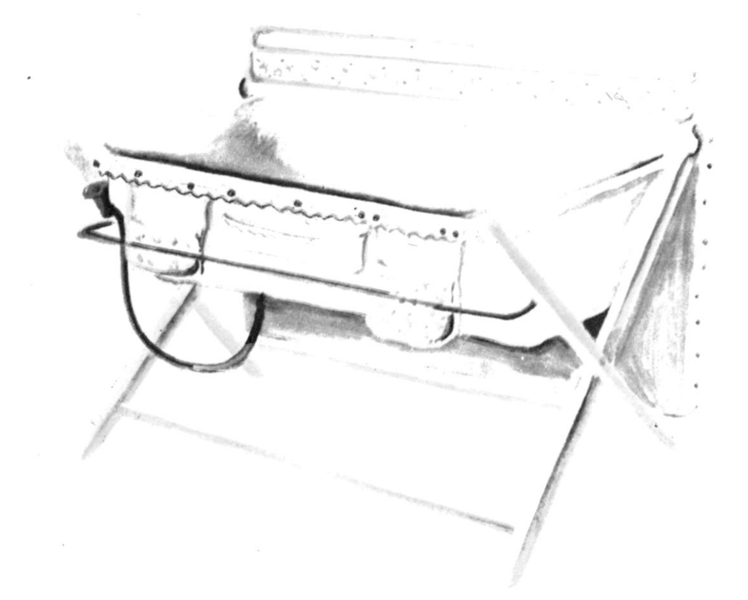

"Aunt Pat is going to help you and Mummy feed and bathe the baby," said Daddy as they watched the train pull into the station.

"There's Aunt Pat," Mike cried.

The first thing Aunt Pat said was, "How big you are, Mike!"

The first thing Mike said was, "We're going to have a baby!"

"Is that so!" said Aunt Pat. She seemed very surprised.

"Yes! And you and I are going to help feed it!"

"Well, well!" said Aunt Pat.

She still looked very surprised.

At supper Mike asked, "Who will bring the baby?"

Daddy said, "No one will bring it. Mummy will go to the hospital for the baby."

"Yes," Mummy explained. "In a little while the doctor will help me have the baby at the hospital."

"Aunt Pat, Mummy's going to have the baby at the hospital," Mike repeated.

That night Mike woke up. The light was burning. It was still dark outside. Aunt Pat was in the hall. She wore her bathrobe. Mummy and Daddy were up, too.

"Where are you going?" Mike asked.

Mummy kissed Mike and smiled. "I'm going to the hospital for our baby," she said. "I'll bring it home soon."

In the morning Mike helped Aunt Pat. He laced his shoes. He brought out the corn flakes. He carried chairs to the table. He brought in the milk. And he ate every bit of his breakfast.

The telephone rang. Mike got there first. It was Daddy.

Daddy said, "Mike, you have a fine baby sister!"

"Ohhh!" said Mike, handing the telephone to Aunt Pat. "Maybe I could run and tell Mrs. Blair."

"Of course you may," Aunt Pat told him.

So Mike ran next door as fast as he could.

Before long Daddy came home in the car. He boosted Mike in the air and then ran into the house to see Aunt Pat.

Just then a big red truck stopped in front of the house. The delivery man took a big box from the truck. He was bringing it to Mike's house. What could it be?

It wasn't Christmas yet, so it couldn't be a Christmas present. It couldn't be a lawn mower. Daddy still had a lawn mower. And it couldn't be a tricycle. Mike still had his red tricycle. Could it be another bathinette?

Mike ran up the steps. He didn't even wait to say "Hello" to the delivery man. He went looking for Daddy and Aunt Pat. He was quite excited.

"Aunt Pat," Mike said, "are we going to have ANOTHER baby?"

"What!" said Daddy.

"I hardly think so," said Aunt Pat. "At least not for a while. Why do you ask?"

"Well," said Mike, "the delivery man is here with another box. He brought one just before the baby came!"

Daddy laughed and said, "This is a surprise for YOU, Mikie. Let's go and get the package."

The delivery man was at the door.

"Hello," Mike said.

"Hello, there," said the delivery man.

"That's for ME," Mike told him and pointed to the big package. Daddy and the delivery man carried the box up the stairs.

"What can it be?" Mike wondered. "It's too big to be toys."

"Come on!" said Daddy.

"Give me a hand and soon you'll see what it is."

Mike ran upstairs. He and Daddy opened the box and there—was a big new bed!

"For me!" cried Mike.

Mike and Daddy put it together. Mike was very happy, and said, "NOW the baby can have my little bed!"

He wanted very much to see the baby.

It seemed a very long time that he had to wait. Aunt Pat and Daddy went to see Mummy and the baby every day.

Mike spent the days finding some of his toys for the baby to play with when she came home. What *would* she be like?

"What will we call her?" he wondered.

Daddy and Mike decided to call the baby Pat after Aunt Pat.

All the time Mike wondered, Where will she want to play? What will the baby look like? When will Mummy and the baby come home?

Then one day Daddy was bringing Mummy and Pat home from the hospital in the car. Mike sat on the steps and waited for them. A green car came along. It was not the car that Mike was looking for. A yellow car came along. It was not the right car either.

Then a blue car turned the corner. That was their car.

Mike ran down the sidewalk to the car. Daddy got out first. He gave Mike an extra high boost in the air. Mummy kissed Mike and told him how glad she was to be home.

Mrs. Blair came over from the house next door. Mrs. Mooney and Mrs. Hansen walked over from their houses across the street. Everyone wanted to see little Pat.

But Mike wanted to see her most of all. He looked. She had tiny hands, and she had blue eyes. She had soft yellow hair, just as he had thought she might.

When Aunt Pat, Daddy, little Pat, and Mummy were inside, Mike said, "May I hold our baby?"

"Of course you may," Mummy said.

So Mike sat on the couch. Then they put a big pillow on his lap and put the baby on the pillow. How proud Mike was! It's wonderful to have a baby, Mike decided.

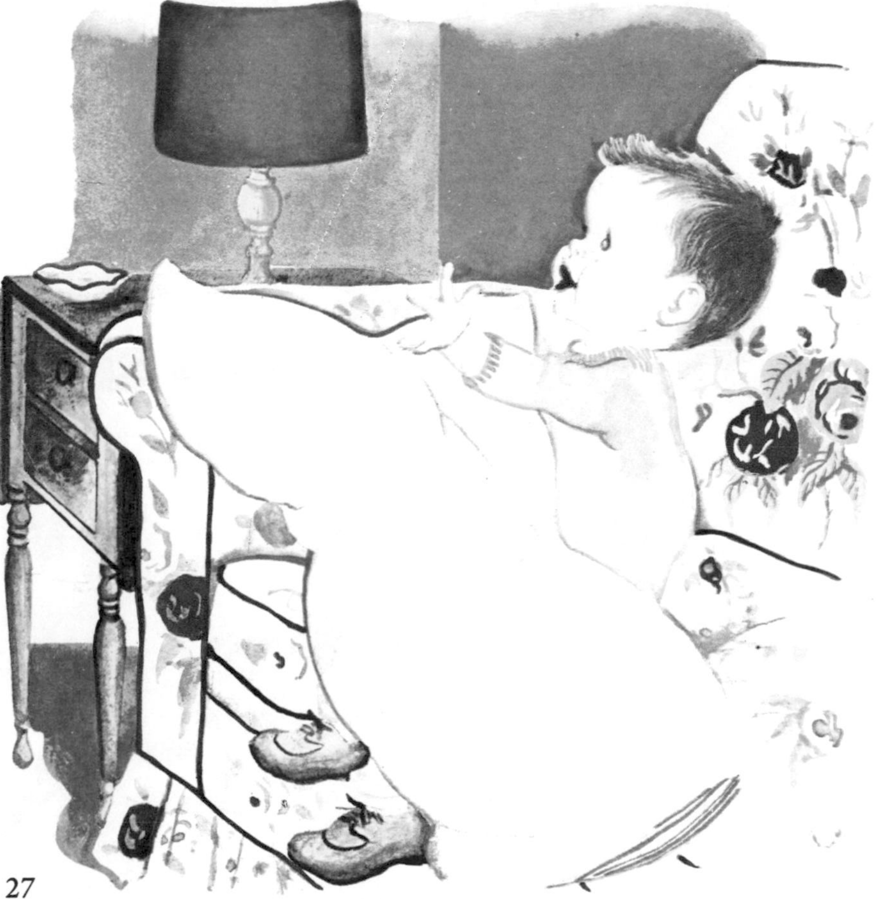

SCUFFY THE TUGBOAT

and His Adventures Down the River

By Gertrude Crampton

WITH PICTURES BY TIBOR GERGELY

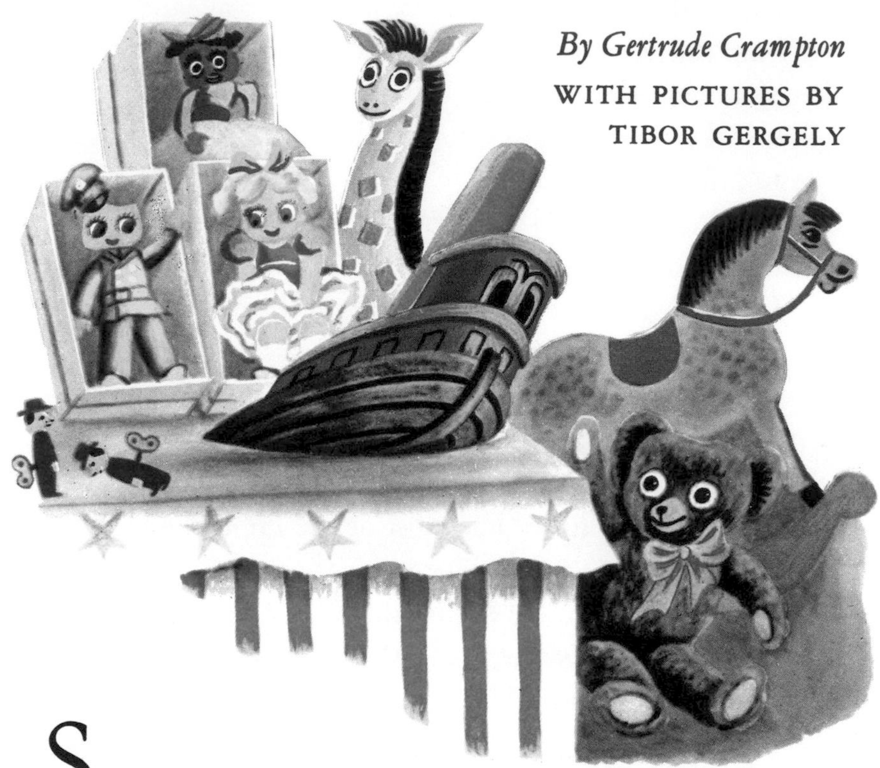

SCUFFY was sad. Scuffy was cross. Scuffy sniffed his blue smokestack.

"A toy store is no place for a red-painted tugboat," said Scuffy, and he sniffed his blue smokestack again. "I was meant for bigger things."

"Perhaps you would not be cross if you went sailing," said the man with the polka dot tie, who owned the shop.

So one night he took Scuffy home to his little boy. He filled the bathtub with water.

"Sail, little tugboat," said the little boy.

"I won't sail in a bathtub," said Scuffy. "A tub is no place for a red-painted tugboat. I was meant for bigger things."

The next day the man with the polka dot tie and his little boy carried Scuffy to a laughing brook that started high in the hills.

"Sail, little tugboat," said the man with the polka dot tie.

It was Spring, and the brook was full to the brim with its water. And the water moved in a hurry, as all things move in a hurry when it is Spring.

Scuffy was in a hurry, too.

"Come back little tugboat, come back," cried the little boy as the hurrying, brimful brook carried Scuffy downstream.

"Not I," tooted Scuffy. "Not I. This is the life for me."

All that day Scuffy sailed along with the brook.

Past the meadows filled with cowslips. Past the women washing clothes on the bank. Past the little woods filled with violets.

Cows came to the brook to drink.

They stood in the cool water, and it was fun to sail around between their legs and bump softly into their noses.

It was fun to see them drink.

But when a white and brown cow almost drank Scuffy instead of the brook's cool water, Scuffy was frightened. That was not fun!

Night came, and with it the moon.

There was nothing to see but the quiet trees.

Suddenly an owl called out, "Hoot, hooot!"

"Toot, tooot!" cried the frightened tugboat, and he wished he could see the smiling, friendly face of the man with the polka dot tie.

When morning came, Scuffy was cross instead of frightened.

"I was meant for bigger things, but which way am I to go?" he said. But there was only one way to go, and that was with the running water where the two brooks met to form a small river. And with the river sailed Scuffy, the red-painted tugboat.

He was proud when he sailed past villages.

"People build villages at the edge of my river," said Scuffy, and he straightened his blue smokestack.

Once Scuffy's river joined a small one jammed with logs. Here were men in heavy jackets and great boots, walking about on the floating logs, trying to pry them free.

"Toot, toot, let me through," demanded Scuffy. But the men paid no attention to him. They pushed the logs apart so they would drift with the river to the sawmill in the town.

Scuffy bumped along with the jostling logs.

"Ouch!" he cried as two logs bumped together.

"This is a fine river," said Scuffy, "but it's very busy and very big for me."

He was proud when he sailed under the bridges.

"My river is so wide and so deep that people must build bridges to cross it."

The river moved through big towns now instead of villages.

And the bridges over it were very wide—wide enough so that many cars and trucks and streetcars could cross all at once.

The river got deeper and deeper. Scuffy did not have to tuck up his bottom.

The river moved faster and faster.

"I feel like a train instead of a tugboat," said Scuffy, as he was hurried along.

He was proud when he passed the old sawmill with its water wheel.

But high in the hills and mountains the winter snow melted. Water filled the brooks and rushed from there into the small rivers. Faster and faster it flowed, to the great river where Scuffy sailed.

"There is too much water in this river," said Scuffy, as he pitched and tossed on the waves. "Soon it will splash over the top and what a flood there will be!"

Soon great armies of men came to save the fields and towns from the rushing water.

They filled bags with sand and put them at the edge of the river.

"They're making higher banks for the river," shouted Scuffy, "to hold the water back." The water rose higher and higher.

The men built the sand bags higher and higher. Higher! went the river. Higher! went the sand bags.

At last the water rose no more. The flood water rushed on to the sea, and Scuffy raced along with the flood. The people and the fields and the towns were safe.

On went the river to the sea. At last Scuffy sailed into a big city. Here the river widened, and all about were docks and wharves.

Oh, it was a busy place and a noisy place! The cranes groaned as they swung the cargoes into great ships. The porters shouted as they carried suitcases and boxes on board.

Horses stamped and truck motors roared, streetcars clanged and people shouted. Scuffy said, "Toot, toot," but nobody noticed.

"Oh, oh!" cried Scuffy when he saw the sea. "There is no beginning and there is no end to the sea. I wish I could find the man with the polka dot tie and his little boy!"

Just as the little red-painted tugboat sailed past the last piece of land, a hand reached out and picked him up. And there was the man with the polka dot tie, with his little boy beside him.

Scuffy is home now with the man with the polka dot tie and his little boy.

He sails from one end of the bathtub to the other.

"This is the place for a red-painted tugboat," says Scuffy. "And this is the life for me."

FIX IT, PLEASE!

BY LUCY SPRAGUE MITCHELL

Pictures by Eloise Wilkin

POLLY was a little girl. And Jimmy was a little boy, but not quite as little as Polly.

Polly and Jimmy had the same mother. And Polly and Jimmy had the same daddy. They were brother and sister.

One day Polly fell down. And her button popped right off her overalls. Polly picked up the button and ran fast, fast to Mother.

"Fix it, Mommy, please," said Polly.

So her mother sewed the button on tight.

"It's all fixed," smiled Polly. "Thank you."

One day Jimmy and Polly were eating their luncheon. Jimmy jumped up in a hurry and bang! His plate fell right on the floor and broke in two.

Jimmy picked up the two pieces of the plate.

"Mommy, Mommy!" he called. "Fix my plate—it's broken. Please fix it."

"Bring me the bottle of glue, Jimmy," called his mother.

Mother took a little brush and swished the sticky glue on the edge of one piece of the broken plate. And she swished the sticky glue on the edge of the other piece. Then she pushed the two pieces together tight and put the plate away for the glue to dry.

The next day Jimmy looked at his plate.

"It has a little line down the middle of it like a crack," said Jimmy. "But anyway, it's fixed. Thank you, Mother."

Pat, pat, pat ran Polly's feet, and rattle, rattle, rattled the wagon Polly was pulling. Then whang! the wagon ran into the fence and off rolled a wheel. Polly began to cry, for she was a very little girl. Then she stopped crying and ran to find her Daddy.

"My wagon broke," she said. "Fix it, please, Daddy."

So Daddy got a nut and some pliers. He put a part of the wagon through the hole in the wheel and turned and turned the nut till the wheel was tight on the wagon again.

"It's all fixed," said Polly. "It runs again."

One day Jimmy knocked his chair over. The chair fell with a crash and one of the legs broke.

"Daddy!" yelled Jimmy. "My chair is broken. Please try to fix it."

So Daddy got his tools—a saw, a hammer and some nails. He took a new piece of wood and sawed it just the right size for a new leg for the chair. Then he nailed the new leg on the chair—bang, bang!

One day Jimmy called, "You can't catch me!"

Polly ran fast, fast after Jimmy. Jimmy ran fast, fast away from Polly. He ran so fast he fell flat. He hurt his knee. His knee began to bleed. Jimmy began to cry. Polly began to cry too, for she was a very little girl.

Their mother came running fast. She saw Jimmy's knee. First she kissed him. Then she said, "We'll fix your knee, Jimmy."

First she washed Jimmy's knee until there was no dirt left. Then she painted iodine on his knee. The knee looked bright yellow. Then she put a bandage on his knee and fastened the bandage with some sticky tape.

Little Polly watched it all.

"I want a bandage, too," she said.

So Mother cut off a little piece of sticky tape and put it on Polly's knee.

"Now you're both all fixed up," said Mother.

Jimmy sat down in the chair.

"It's all fixed," he said. "I can sit on it."

Polly had a rag doll named Dear-Anne. One day Dear-Anne's arm came right off. "Dear-Anne has lost her arm," wailed Polly.

So Mother brought her needle and thread. She sewed Dear-Anne's arm on again.

"Dear-Anne is all fixed," said Polly.

And she gave Dear-Anne a big kiss.

Jimmy's play suit had no buttons. It had a zipper. Jimmy could pull the zipper up—zzzzzip! One day the zipper stuck. It wouldn't pull up.

He ran to Mother calling, "My zipper's broken."

"Zippers are hard to fix, Jimmy," said Mother.

She took her scissors and she fussed and fussed with the zipper.

"Now try it, Jimmy," she said.

Z,z,zzzzzip! It pulled up.

"It's fixed!" cried Jimmy.

One day Polly and Jimmy and Daddy and Mother got into their old car. Burrrrr, the car began to shake. Then off they went, whizzing down the road.

All of a sudden, the car began to bump. It bumped and bumped though there weren't any bumps in the road.

"We've got a flat tire," said Daddy, and he sounded very mad.

"We'll get out while you fix it," said Mother.

So Daddy got out the jack and put it under the car. He moved the jack up and down until the back wheels were off the ground. Then he took the flat tire off. He took the spare tire out of the back of the car and put it on. Then he took the jack out from under the car. His hands were dirty, his trousers were dirty, his face was dirty.

"I hate to change a tire," he said.

One day Jimmy felt sick. Then Polly felt sick. Mother put them both to bed. Then she went to the telephone and called the doctor.

"Doctor," she said, "Jimmy and Polly are sick. Will you come to see them?"

The doctor came. He had a little black bag.

"Open your mouth and say 'Ah,'" said the doctor.

He looked at Jimmy's tongue and took his temperature. He looked at Polly's tongue and took her temperature. Then he opened his little black bag and took out some pink medicine.

"Here, Jimmy," said the doctor. "This pink medicine will fix you up in no time."

Jimmy swallowed the pink medicine.

"Here is yours now, Polly," said the doctor.

Polly swallowed the pink medicine.

The doctor was right. The next day Jimmy and Polly felt as frisky as two little puppies.

"Do you know what I am going to be when I am big?" said Jimmy to Polly.

"What?" said Polly.

"The fix-it man," said Jimmy.

"And I'll be the fix-it mommy," said Polly.

NOISES AND MR. FLIBBERTY-JIB

BY GERTRUDE CRAMPTON

ILLUSTRATED BY
ELOISE WILKIN

MR. FLIBBERTY-JIB had a most unusual rumble in his head. It went *rumble-rumble-rumble,* and then it went **bumble-bumble-bumble.**

Now, Mrs. Flibberty-jib didn't mean to, but she made Mr. Flibberty-jib's rumble and bumble worse than ever.

You see, Mrs. Flibberty-jib cooks the very finest roast beef in town. But no one can cook roast beef without closing the oven door **ker-shut** and covering the roasting pans ***ker-bang.***

Besides, Mrs. Flibberty-jib knits mittens all day long. And no one can knit even one mitten unless the needles say, **"Click, click, clickety click!** Click and knit! Knit and click."

Mrs. Flibberty-jib says that Mr. Flibberty-jib has a rumble in his head because he eats too little roast beef and doesn't wear his mittens.

He says he has a large rumble in his head because the house and town are full of noises.

She says, "Nonsense!"

Then the old clock strikes, **"Bong, bong, bong!** Three o'clock, Mr. Flibberty-jib."

The telephone shouts, ***"Brr-ring! Brr-ring!*** Answer me. Quick, answer me!"

The grocery boy at the back door says, **"TAP, TAP, TAP!** Answer *me!"*

And then the telephone rings again.

"Too much noise," says Mr. Flibberty-jib.

The gray mouse that lives in the kitchen wall peeks out of the mouse hole.

"Cheese!" says the gray mouse to herself, and scampers softly over the floor like a gray shadow.

But Mrs. Flibberty-jib sees her.

"Eeeeee!" screams Mrs. Flibberty-jib.

"Squee!" squeaks little gray mouse.

"See?" says Mr. Flibberty-jib. "Too much noise."

"Nonsense!" says Mrs. Flibberty-jib, and gets off the chair.

Well, says Mr. Flibberty-jib, suppose he goes downtown to buy some red yarn for Mrs. Flibberty-jib's mittens.

The first things he hears is—

CLANG! CLANG! CLANG!

Then, says Mr. Flibberty-jib, he walks to the curb and gets ready to cross the street. He looks to left and right. Then he puts his left foot down. And around the corner comes—

Beep! Beep! Beep!

Then, says Mr. Flibberty-jib, he walks to the curb and gets ready to cross the street again. He looks to left and right. Then he puts his right foot down.

And around the corner comes—

CLOP, CLOP, CLOPPETY, CLOP!

"It is no wonder," says Mr. Flibberty-jib, "that my head rumbles.

"Every time—not just once-in-a-time—I go to buy red yarn, the policeman blows his whistle,

Whee-ee-ee-ee-ee!

"The fire engine races by me, **OO-oo-oo-OO-oo-oo-oo-OO-oo-OO!**

"And when I get home again, the front door always, always slips out of my hand and goes—***BANG!***"

"You should eat your roast beef, Mr. Flibberty-jib," said Mrs. Flibberty-jib, as she often did, "and wear your mittens."

"Nonsense!" shouted Mr. Flibberty-jib, giving his umbrella a good hard bump. "The noise! It's the noise!"

"Roast beef and mittens," said Mrs. Flibberty-jib.

"Noise!" roared Mr. Flibberty-jib.

This went on for days and days and days. Mrs. Flibberty-jib went on roasting the finest roast beef in the town. She went on making mittens—red mittens, blue mittens, yellow mittens.

Mr. Flibberty-jib's rumble in his head went on rumbling. At last Mr. Flibberty-jib came home in a rage.

"I can't stand this *rumble-rumble-rumble* and **bumble-bumble-bumble,**" he said. "We will go to the country where it is quiet. Everyone knows the country is quiet and a very good place for rumbles and bumbles."

"Very well, Mr. Flibberty-jib," said Mrs. Flibberty-jib.

So Mr. Flibberty-jib packed up his brown shoes and his blue suit and his red tie. He put his hat over the rumble in his head. And he was ready to go to the country.

Mrs. Flibberty-jib packed up her roasting pans and her knitting needles and yarn. And she was ready to go to the country.

Poor Mr. Flibberty-jib! The train whistle said, **"TOOT, TOOT, TOOT,"** all the way to the country.

And every crossing bell said, **"Ting-ting-and-a-little-ting,"** all the way to the country.

But at last Mr. Flibberty-jib and Mrs. Flibberty-jib got to the country.

Mr. Flibberty-jib unpacked his brown shoes and his blue suit and his red tie and went for a quiet walk. Mrs. Flibberty-jib unpacked her roasting pans and her knitting needles and her yarn and began to cook a fine roast of beef.

They were so tired from all the packing and unpacking that they went to bed as soon as they had eaten supper.

"Oh, this is the life!" said Mr. Flibberty-jib, who hadn't eaten any of the roast beef.

Poor Mr. Flibberty-jib! He had just turned off the light and closed his eyes, when—

"Whoo? Who? Who?"

Poor, poor Mr. Flibberty-jib!

He was sure he had just hopped into bed.

He was sure he had just gone to sleep.

He was sure it was just the beginning of the night, when— "Cock-a-doodle-doo! Cock-a-doodle-doo!"

Mr. Flibberty-jib ran down the stairs and out of the house.

"Ssh! Sssh!" he said to the rooster. "I am a poor man with a rumble and bumble in my head."

"Cock-a-doodle-doo!"

shouted the rooster.

And the hens said,

"Cluck, cluck, cluck!"

"Oh, my!" cried Mr. Flibberty-jib. "What next?"

These were next:

"BOW, WOW, WOW!"

"Meow, meow, meow!"

Then the ducks came a-waddling to find a place for swimming. "QUACK, QUACK, QUACK!"

The old windmill turned and turned in the wind. It pumped water, and the horse came to drink.

"Squee-gee, squee-gee, squee-gee!" said the windmill. "I must turn and turn. Soon Bossy will come for her drink of cold water. Blow me around and around, Wind. *Squee-gee, squee-gee, squee-gee!"*

And the Bob White called from the green field,

"Bob *white!* Bob *white!*"

The big Bossy cow said, "MOO-OOO! MOO-OO!" It was time for milking!

The milk pails went **clank-clankety-clank** as the farmer's biggest boy carried them into the barn.

And Mr. Flibberty-jib's head went *rumble-rumble-rumble* from his left ear to his right ear, and **bumble-bumble-bumble** from his right ear to his left ear.

"Less noise!" shouted Mr. Flibberty-jib.

"More roast beef," said Mrs. Flibberty-jib. "And your mittens."

"Well, now, it may be that you are right," said Mr. Flibberty-jib. "I hope so, for I have found that, town or country, there will always be—

NOISES! NOISES! NOISES!

So Mr. Flibberty-jib sat down at the table, and first he ate a small piece of roast beef and then a very large piece of roast beef.

And in the afternoon he was pleased to find that the **bumble-bumble-bumble** was gone from his head.

The next day he ate two very large pieces of roast beef and a slice of bread covered with rich brown gravy.

When he went outdoors, he wore the red-and-yellow mittens Mrs. Flibberty-jib had very kindly made for him.

And he was pleased to find that the *rumble-rumble-rumble* was gone from his head.

"Fine place, the country," said Mr. Flibberty-jib that night as he watched the big round moon.

He listened to the owl asking, **"Who? Whoo?"**

And not a **bumble-bumble-bumble** did Mr. Flibberty-jib hear.

"Fine place, the country," said Mr. Flibberty-jib next morning, and he jumped out of bed before the sun was up.

When the black rooster hurried sleepily to the fence to crow the sun up, there was Mr. Flibberty-jib.

"Cock-a-doodle-DOo!"

"Listen to me try it," said Mr. Flibberty-jib.

"COCK-A-DOODLE-DOO!"

"Very good," said the black rooster. "Now listen to me."

He took a deep, DEEP breath.

And not a *rumble-rumble-rumble* did Mr. Flibberty-jib hear.

Now Mr. Flibberty-jib and Mrs. Flibberty-jib go to the country every summer, and to the big city every winter.

And from that day to this, Mr. Flibberty-jib has always eaten plenty of roast beef, and he always wears his red-and-yellow mittens—except, of course, when he is eating roast beef.

And not a *rumble-rumble-rumble* —or a **bumble-bumble-bumble** —does Mr. Flibberty-jib ever hear.

BUSY TIMMY

BY KATHRYN
and BYRON JACKSON
PICTURES BY
ELOISE WILKIN

1

Timmy is
a big boy.

2

He can put on his outdoor clothes.

3

He can find his shovel
and his big sand pail.

4

He goes down the steps.
No one has to help him.
He's a big boy now.

5

He climbs in his sand-box.

6

robin sees Timmy and comes flying.

7

A squirrel sees Timmy and comes running.

8

A rabbit sees Timmy
and comes hopping.
They all watch Timmy.

9

He makes little holes
and big hills.

10

He rides on his horse
all around the flower bed,

up bumps and down bumps

12

and back home again.

13

Timmy goes up the steps

and opens the door all by himself.

15

He gets ready
for his bath.

No one has to help him.
He's a big boy now.

16

He splashes in the bathtub,
and sails his new boat.

He puts on his own bib,

18

and holds his own cup.

19

He eats all his supper with no help at all.

20

He brushes
his own teeth.

21

He climbs into bed, all by himself!

22

"Hush!" says the robin.

23

"Hush!" says the squirrel.

24

hush!" says the rabbit.
"Timmy is a big boy,
and Timmy is going to sleep!"

25

Yes,
Timmy *is* a big boy—
and he is sound asleep.

26

You are big, too.
Timmy does a lot of things. So can you!

LITTLE Peewee

OR NOW OPEN THE BOX

BY DOROTHY KUNHARDT

PICTURES BY J. P. MILLER

ONCE there was a circus man with a quite tall red hat on his head and he had a circus of his very own so that was why he was called the circus man, and it was a wonderful wonderful wonderful circus.

The circus man kept his wonderful circus inside a big red tent.

Every day the circus man stood in front of his big red tent and every day he held up something in his hand very high for everybody to see. He held up a teeny weeny little box in his hand and he shouted very LOUD . . . Come on everybody come on over here to my tent come on everybody I have something exciting to show you just wait till I show you what I have in this little box so hurry up everybody and everybody came running and skipping and hopping as fast as they could to the circus man's big red tent and when everybody was there the circus man said . . . Everybody look now everybody look now everybody LOOK now everybody LOOK!

Then he opened the box and out came the teeniest-weeniest teeny teeny teeny weeny weeny weeny little dog in all the world and he was dear little Peewee the circus dog.

He just stepped out of his teeny weeny box and he looked around at everybody and the minute he looked around at everybody everybody loved him.

Then the circus man said Well I knew everybody would love my little Peewee it's too bad he doesn't know any tricks not a single one not even how to roll over not even how to shake hands but never mind he is so teeny weeny that everybody loves him. And that was true because EVERYBODY loved little Peewee.

There was the clown with two heads but one of them is probably make-believe.

He loved little Peewee.

There was the small man who could juggle three ducks all at the same time. He loved little Peewee.

There was the man sitting on a chair on top of six tables just going to fall down and blowing soap bubbles. He loved little Peewee.

There was the lady standing on her head on an umbrella and with one foot she is holding a pair of scissors and with the other foot she is holding a cup full of nice warm milk. She loved little Peewee.

There was the elephant crawling under another elephant. He loved little Peewee.

There was the thin man. He loved little Peewee.

There was the strong baby holding up an automobile with a seal in the back seat. He loved little Peewee.

There was the snake that can put his tail in his mouth and then go rolling right up the stairs. He loved little Peewee.

There was the lady hanging in the air just by her nose being tied to a good strong rope. She loved little Peewee.

There was the fat lady. She loved little Peewee.

There was the polar bear who could jump up in the air and click his ice skates together four times.

He loved little Peewee.

There was the goat that can stand right on a bed with the bed all burning up and not even mind about the fire being hot. He loved little Peewee.

There was the huge tall giant.

He loved little Peewee.

But one day a terrible frightful awful thing happened. One day little teeny weeny weeny weeny Peewee started to grow

and he grew

and he grew

and he grew

until poor little Peewee the circus dog was just the same size as any other plain dog that you would see anywhere if you were looking at any plain dog and how could a circus man keep just a plain dog in his circus. Then the circus man cried and he said Now I can't keep you in my circus any more dear little Peewee and I am so sorry if only you could do some tricks it would be different but you can't do any tricks not even roll over not even shake hands and now you are just as big as any plain dog and how can I keep just a plain dog in my circus. NO I just can't so we must say goodbye dear little Peewee.

Then all the whole wonderful circus cried and the whole circus said Goodbye dear little Peewee.

So poor little Peewee started to go away and never come back to the circus any more and JUST THEN a wonderful splendid beautiful thing happened. Just as dear little Peewee was beginning to walk away so sadly and so slowly . . . he started to grow again!

And he grew

and he grew

and he grew

and then the circus man said Oh my dearest little Peewee now you won't have to go after all because now you are so lovely and big you are just the very dog for my circus! So little Peewee stayed in the circus man's wonderful circus and everybody loved him and every day just before the circus started the circus man would stand outside the big red tent and beside him he would have a huge enormous box right beside him so everybody could see what a huge enormous box it was and then the circus man would shout Come on everybody come on over here to my tent hurry up everybody I have something exciting to show you just wait till you see what I have in this great enormous box so hurry up everybody.

And everybody would come running and skipping and hopping to the circus man's wonderful circus tent and then the circus man would say Come on inside the tent everybody and I will open the box for you.

And then everybody would help the circus man push and push the great enormous box into the tent and then the circus man would open the top of the great enormous box and out would POP dear little Peewee and the circus man would say People this is my dear little circus dog Peewee and he is the hugest most enormous dog in the whole world and I love him dearly and every time the circus man said he is the hugest most enormous dog in the whole world and I love him dearly then little Peewee felt

VERY

HAPPY

INDEED!

GOOD MORNING and GOOD NIGHT

Story by Jane Werner
Pictures by Eloise Wilkin

THERE was once a little boy who, strange as it may seem, did not like to get up in the morning—imagine that!

Every day his mother had to call him and call him to wake him, and each day it was harder than it had been the day before.

At last one morning he just would not wake up at all!

His mother called, "Time to get up, Sonny!"

But the little boy did not wake up.

His father called, "Time to roll out, Son!"

But the little boy did not wake up.

His sister and brother called, "Hurry up, lazy bones! We're almost ready for breakfast!"

But still that little boy slept on.

Then his kitten came and jumped on the little boy's head and mewed at him.

But that did not wake him.

His puppy bounced up and down on the little boy's tummy and licked his sleepy face with a quick, wet tongue.

But even that did not wake him.

The parrot from next door perched on his window sill and screeched at him.

And a black panther from the zoo came and snarled most horribly at him.

And a lion roared a great, tremendous roar that shook the walls.

But still that sleepy little boy slept on.

"Well, we've done all we could," said his mother with a sigh.

So they all went downstairs for breakfast.

Close by, while the hall seemed quite empty, out of a little mouse hole down at the floor popped a tiny gray mouse.

The little mouse sat in his doorway and wiggled his whiskers for a moment.

Then, when he was quite certain that everyone was eating breakfast, the little mouse scampered up to the little boy's room, over to the bed, and up onto the little boy's pillow.

He put his pointed little nose very close to the little boy's ear and whispered,

ever so softly,
"Good morning!"

At that the sleepy little boy's eyes popped wide open.

"Good morning to you!" he said. "My, but I'm hungry!"

And he sprang out of bed, and washed and dressed in a flash, and ran down the stairs to breakfast. And the tiny little mouse went, too.

THERE was once a little girl who, strange as it may seem, did not like to go to bed—imagine that!

Every evening she wanted to stay up and play.

And every evening her mother said, "Bedtime, Sister! Hurry and get ready for bed!"

But every evening that little girl replied, "Oh, dear. I am wide awake. I still want to play."

So one evening her mother said, "Very well. You may stay. But I am afraid you will have to play alone.

"Your brothers are going to sleep, and your daddy and I are going to sleep, so you will be all alone. Good night, my little wide-awake girl."

"Good night," said the little girl. "I do not mind being alone. I shall play with my toys."

First she went to her dollhouse.

But her dolls had been playing all day long, and now they were fast asleep.

"Well then," said the little girl to herself, "I will build with the blocks."

So she looked for the blocks, but they were all tucked away for the night.

"Oh," she said.

"Well, I will play with the Noah's ark."

But the Noah's ark was dark and silent.

All the animals two by two were fast asleep, and Mr. and Mrs. Noah were fast asleep, too.

"Well," said the little girl, "I will play with my sleepy doll. She sleeps all day so she must be wide awake at night."

But the sleepy doll was upstairs in the little girl's bedroom.

So the little girl crept very quietly up the stairs, past the room where her brothers were fast asleep, and past the room where her father and mother were fast asleep, and into her own little room.

There was the sleepy doll, safe and sound, but the sleepy doll was fast asleep, too.

And the whole house was so dark and quiet and full of sleep that the little girl's eyes began to feel very heavy.

So she took the sleepy doll in her arms and curled up in her own little bed, and soon that wide-awake little girl was fast asleep, too.

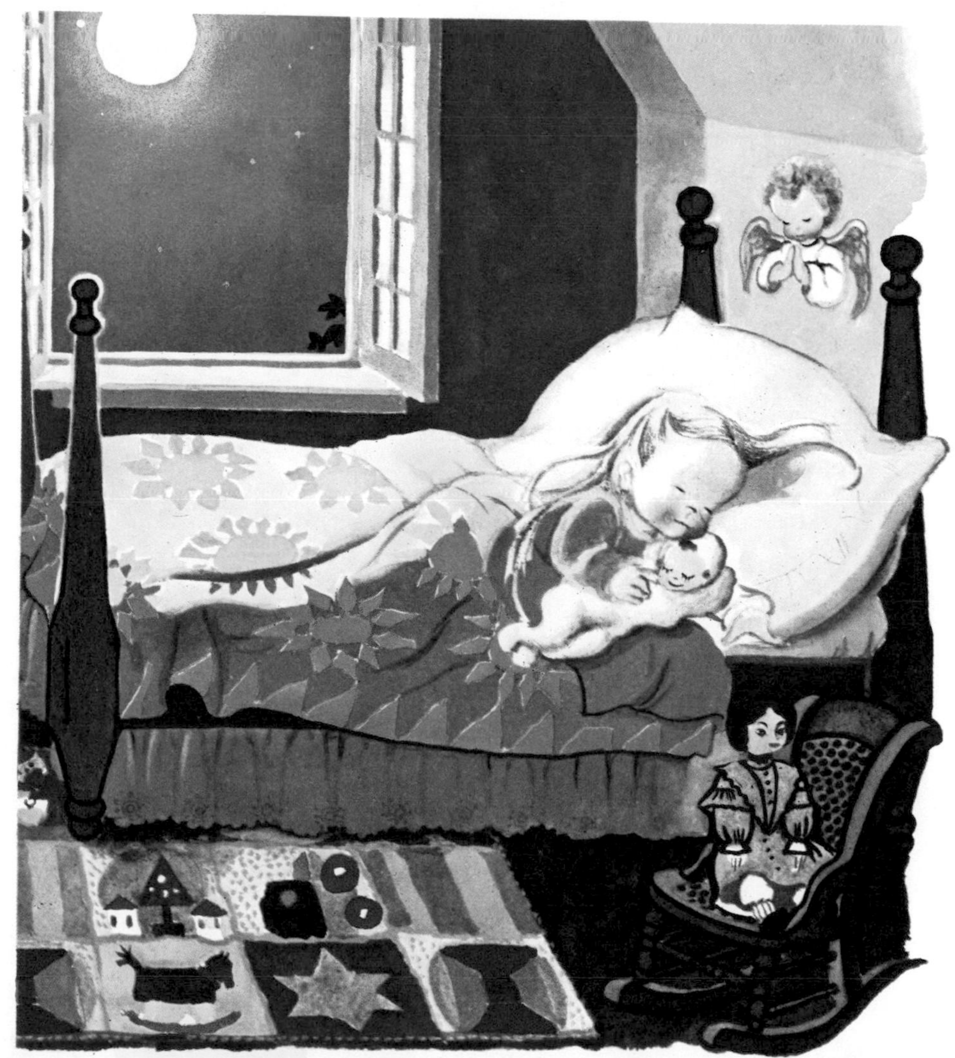

GUESS WHO LIVES HERE

BY LOUISE WOODCOCK

PICTURES BY ELOISE WILKIN

SOMEBODY lives in this house.
He wears green overalls
And a striped sweater.
He likes to ride a bike
And build with blocks.
Guess who it is!
It's Terry.
Somebody else lives in this house.
She has curly hair and she smiles very often.
She wears a dress and sometimes an apron.
She cooks good things to eat
every night,
And she tucks Terry into bed
with a kiss.
Guess who it is!
It's Terry's mother.
Somebody else lives in this house.
He is very tall,
And he walks with long steps.
He goes out to work in the morning
And sometimes he brings Terry a present
when he comes home at night.
Guess who it is!
It's Terry's father.

Somebody else lives in this house.
She is very short.
She can't stand up even holding onto a chair.
She takes her milk out of a bottle.
She has only three teeth.
Guess who it is!
It's Terry's baby sister.

Somebody else lives in this house. He has rough brown hair
and a tail he can wag.
All he can say is "Bow-wow!" or "Woof-woof!"
He loves tc go everywhere
Terry goes.
Guess who it is!
It's Terry's dog Wolfie.
Somebody else lives in this house.
She is soft and furry.
She has claws
that can scratch
but she doesn't scratch
very often.
She drinks milk
from a saucer on the floor.
She likes to sleep
in nice warm places.
Guess who it is!
It's Terry's cat Silkie.
Somebody else lives
in this house.
He is very very tiny
And can run very fast.

He is gray all over and his tail's like a little
sharp spike.
He only comes out at night to hunt for crumbs.
Guess who it is!
It's the mouse in Terry's cellar.
Somebody lives in the big tree
beside this house.
She lives in a nest
that she built on a branch.

She has four blue eggs in that nest.
She sits on the nest to keep the eggs warm,
Because her babies are inside them.
Guess who it is!
It's a mother robin.
Somebody else lives in the tree by the house.
He has long gray fur
And a beautiful wavy tail.
He can jump very far from one branch to another.
He loves to eat nuts in his tiny sharp claws.
Guess who it is!
It's a squirrel.
Sometimes somebody comes to this house
before anyone in it is awake.
He doesn't ring the doorbell.
He sets down some bottles on the porch.
He picks up the empty bottles Terry's mother
has put there.
Then he goes on to the house next door.
Guess who it is!
It's the milkman on Terry's street.
Sometimes somebody rings the doorbell
of this house. 
He wears a blue suit.
He carries a big heavy bag on his back.
He takes letters out of his bag,
And puts them in the box beside the front door.
Guess who it is!
It's the postman on Terry's street.
Some days something comes down from the sky—
"Patter-pit-patter!" it says on the roof.
"Splashity-splash!" it says on the walk.
The flowers in the window box shine with wetness,
And all the leaves on the big tree drip.
Guess what it is!
It's the rain.
But most days there's something shining down
on this house.
It makes the flowers in the window box grow.
It makes all the people say to each other,
"What a very nice day it is today!"
Guess what it is!
It's the sunshine.
Sometimes something blows round and round
this house.
It says "Whoo-oo!" in the chimney.
It rattles the windows.
It swings the nest on the branch of the tree.
Guess what it is!
It's the wind.
Sometimes at night something shines on this house.
It isn't warm like the sun.
Sometimes it's a thin little silver curve.
Sometimes it looks like half of a cookie.
Sometimes it's big and round and shines
like a mirror.
It shines on the squirrel in his little tree house.
It shines on the robin in her nest on the branch.
It shines on Terry's baby sister in her crib—
And on Terry's father and mother fast asleep.
It shines in the window at the mouse on
the floor—
And at Silkie too sleepy to chase him.
It shines on Terry—
And on Wolfie stretched out on the floor.
Guess what it is!
It's the moon!

THE SEVEN *Sneezes*

by OLGA CABRAL

Pictures by TIBOR GERGELY

THERE were once a bunny, a kitten and a dog who lived together in a back yard.

The bunny was white, with long, fluffy ears.

The kitten was black, and like all kittens it had teeny ears.

The dog was a great big dog with a great big bark.

Everybody was happy, everybody was satisfied. The bunny loved his big ears, the kitten was glad that hers were tiny, and the dog was proud of his great big bark.

One day a rag man came along in an old wagon. "Any rags today? Any rags today?" sang the rag man.

It was a chilly day. The rag man started to sneeze—

"Any r-ah-ah-ah-ah-"

The bunny, the kitten and the dog all held their breath until the rag man finished his sneeze—

"A-choo! A-cha! A-chachoo!"

They were three hearty sneezes. So hearty, that the rag man was blown out of sight down the road—wagon and horse and all!

"Goodness gracious—" the bunny, the kitten and the dog started to say to each other. And then they saw something strange had happened to them!

The white bunny had the kitten's teeny black ears.

"Why, how silly you both look!" said the dog.

The black kitten had the bunny's long, white ears.

The next minute, he felt silly. Because, when he opened his mouth no great big bark came out. Instead, his voice was only a teeny weeny little meow.

Things were certainly mixed up!

The bunny felt his short, teeny ears. He squeaked.

The kitten felt her long, overgrown ears.

"Goodness gracious me!" she said.

But she said it in a terrible, great big bark! And she fell over backward, so surprised was she to hear herself barking.

Then the kitten saw her teeny ears on the bunny's head. "Give me back my ears!" she said.

She ran over to the bunny and tried to pull them off.

The bunny saw his long ears on the kitten's head.

"Give me back my ears!" he said.

He tried to pull them off too.

And the dog ran around them, meowing like a cat.

"Oh, dear!" barked the cat. "What happened to us?"

"Everything was fine," meowed the dog, "until the rag man came."

The bunny had hiccups, he was so upset.

"The—sneezes—did—it!" he said between hiccups.

They brought him a drink of water.

"Now what are we going to do?" said the dog in his baby-kitten voice.

They thought and thought and then the bunny said, "We must find the rag man."

"And make him put everything back the way it was," said the dog. "If he can!"

So they set out to find the rag man.

Soon they met a goose without any feathers. She was carrying all her feathers in a little basket.

"Pardon us," said the bunny, the cat, and the dog, "but did you see a rag man go by this way?"

"Can't you see that he did?" asked the goose, angrily stamping her foot. "He sneezed off all my feathers! And I'm going to find him and make him put them back on again—if he can!"

So they all went along together.

Pretty soon they met a rooster carrying his comb in his beak. His tail feathers grew on top of his head.

"Pardon us," said the bunny, the cat, the dog, and the pink goose, "but did you see—"

"That awful rag man!" said the rooster angrily. "It's wicked to go around sneezing folk's combs off! I'm going to make him put it back again—if he can!"

So they all went along together.

And pretty soon they met a little girl standing in the road, curling her toes and crying after two long braids had been sneezed right off her head!

So she and the animals all went along together.

Pretty soon they met a little boy, who looked queer because he was wearing only half a jacket, and only one

shoe. He held the other half of his jacket, and the other shoe was stuck very tightly upside down on his head.

"So you've been sneezed at too?" the little boy said to the animals and the little girl. "Let's find that rag man," he said, "and make him fix us up—if he can!"

So they all went along together, and walked and walked until they came to a tumble-down house with an old horse and wagon standing in front. And inside the house someone sneezed—**"Kerchaya!"**

The sneeze blew the horse and wagon up into the air. They came down again on the roof of the tumble-down house.

"This is the right place all right!" said the little boy. So the funny animals and the queer little boy and girl ran into the rag man's house and crowded around him.

"What will my mother say when I tell her I've lost my pigtails?" cried the little girl.

"They'll laugh at me in school with a shoe on my head!" cried the little boy.

"No one will love me with these little ears!" squeaked the bunny.

"Or me with these big ears!" barked the cat.

"How can I guard the house without my great big bark?" meowed the dog.

"I'll freeze without my feathers!" cried the goose.

"No barnyard will have me!" cried the rooster.

"Please don't be angry, my dears," said the rag man. "I guess my sneezes must be magic. I will do my best to sneeze everything right again."

So the rag man sat down to sneeze a magic sneeze.

"Just sprinkle a little pepper on my nose to help," he said.

So the little girl poured a BIG swish of pepper on the rag man's nose, and suddenly— **"Choo! Buttonmyshoe! Switcheroo!"** the rag man sneezed.

The furniture flew out of the window! The house lifted into the air! So did the horse and wagon. So did the fence. And they all came down with a bang in an utterly different place, a much nicer place than before.

"More pepper!" gasped the rag man. The little girl threw the can of pepper at him. Then—

"Katchoo!" The bunny's ears and the kitten's ears flew into the air and came down in their right places!!

"Katchim!" The dog jumped up and barked!!

"Katcham!" The kitten mewed.

"Katchibble!" The feathers in the little basket flew onto the goose again!

"Jiddle-Jaddle!" The little girl's pigtails were back on her head.

"Skedaddle!" The little boy's jacket and shoes were where they should be!

"Jumadiddle!" The rooster's comb flew onto his head and his tail feathers stuck where tail feathers should grow!

Everything was back the way it was!

Then suddenly the rag man looked sneezy again.

"Run," he cried. "Run while I hold my nose!"

So everyone ran all the way home before the rag man could sneeze again.

LITTLE *Yip-Yip* AND HIS BARK

BY KATHRYN AND BYRON JACKSON
ILLUSTRATED BY TIBOR GERGELY

One morning, a very small puppy woke up in a brand-new doghouse.

He sniffed at the cozy, dark inside . . . and he licked at the bright blue outside.

Then he blinked his eyes and looked all around the big busy barnyard.

"It's a wonderful place," he said to himself, "but oh, my, isn't it big?"

Just as he said that, all the big barnyard animals came running up to him.

"Are you the new watchdog?" asked the ducks. The little puppy liked that watchdog idea. He smiled and wagged his tail.

"I guess I am!" he said.

"Well then," crowed the big rooster, "let's hear your big watchdog bark!"

The puppy stood up tall and opened his mouth.

He took a deep breath.

And he barked, "Yip-yip-yip!"

The rooster turned to the pigs. "Did you hear anything?" he asked.

"We heard *something*," squealed the pigs. "It sounded like a squeaky shoe!"

And the calf said she thought it sounded like a baby robin calling its mother.

All the animals laughed and ran away very busily, and the puppy went into his new house.

"Maybe my barking isn't all it should be," he said, and he ran out in the sunshine to practice.

But before he had time for one yip, a great big black dog came bounding up.

That big dog tasted the puppy's milk, and he nibbled the puppy's biscuit.

"Puppy food!" he snorted. "I'll come back when you have some real food for me to eat up!"

And he walked away with his head in the air.

The little puppy felt so cross that he barked until that big dog was out of sight.

"Yip-yip-yip!" he barked.

A little field mouse, on its way to the corn crib, heard that little bark. It jumped when it heard the first yip, but when it heard the second and third it sat down and laughed until the tears dripped off its whiskers.

"Oh, ho, ho!" laughed the mouse. "I have baby mice at home who can bark louder than that!"

"Is that so!" cried the puppy. He ran at the mouse with all his sharp little teeth showing.

"I'll bite you into three pieces!" he barked, and he chased the mouse across the barnyard.

"I'll bite—"

But the mouse was gone! It had disappeared through the cracks in the corn crib, and the puppy was chasing nobody at all.

"Well," he barked proudly, "I guess I scared *him* all right!"

And then he heard all the mice in the corn crib barking little tiny barks.

"Yip-yip-yip," they laughed. "Yip-yip! Oh, what a watchdog!"

He looked for something bigger to scare.

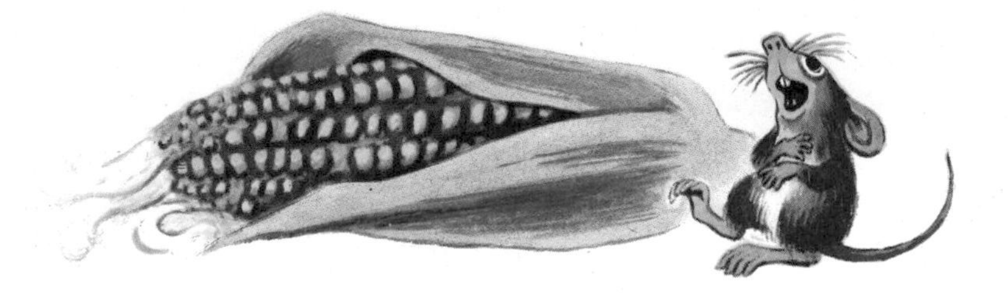

And just as it was getting dark he saw something *much* bigger.

A slim, sly, red fox came creeping into the barnyard. He slithered straight toward the hen house, and he looked so mean and hungry that the little puppy backed away from him.

"I'll have to bark louder than ever this time," he whispered bravely, and he backed right into an empty milk pail. "You have to bark very loud to scare a fox."

The sly fox crept nearer and nearer and nearer to the hen house, licking his chops and snickering to himself. And then, all at once, the puppy took a deep breath and barked.

When that little bark came out of the milk pail, it wasn't a little yip-yip-yip at all! It echoed and rumbled around in the pail, and when it came out, it was a fine big bark.

It went: BOW-WOW-WOW! and it was so loud that the puppy jumped in the air, pail and all.

"Help!" squeaked the fox. He turned head over heels, and away he ran as fast as he could go.

The puppy picked himself up and barked a little yip-yip.

He ran back into the pail and barked a big BOW-WOW.

"Now I know how to scare the wits out of anything!" he cried. "All I have to do is hide in an empty something before I bark!"

And he trotted back to his brand-new house with his little tail wagging so fast that it looked like a pinwheel.

Early the next morning, a family of very hungry rabbits hopped into the farm garden.

They chewed tunnels in the biggest cabbages, and hopped through the tunnels. They bit big holes in the middle-sized cabbages, and little holes in the tiny little cabbages.

"Rabbits in the cabbage patch!" the rooster crowed. "Spoiling the whole cabbage patch!"

The little puppy woke up with a start. He ran across the barnyard and into the garden, barking his little yip-yip-yip.

And the rabbits stopped eating just long enough to swallow what they had in their mouths.

Then they jumped up and down on a row of young cabbages, laughing at that sleepy little bark.

"Oh, bad!" yipped the puppy. He started toward his milk pail. And then he said, "Oh, good!" and scampered into an empty barrel that was lying at the edge of the cabbage patch.

"Now for my best rabbit-scaring bark!" thought the little puppy. He closed his eyes and puffed out his chest and barked as loudly as he could.

The big, echoey barrel rolled the sound out, big and loud, into the garden.

BOW WOW

WOW WOW

WOW WOW!!

It came out such a big BOW-WOW-WOW that the rabbits' ears stood on end.

"Watchdogs!" they cried. "At least four great big ones!"

They hopped lickety-split out of the cabbage patch and over the fence. In one second there wasn't a rabbit to be seen!

"That was even better than the milk pail!" laughed the little puppy.

Then he thought he might find something still louder. He nosed all around the farm, barking in every empty thing he found.

He barked in a rusty milk can.

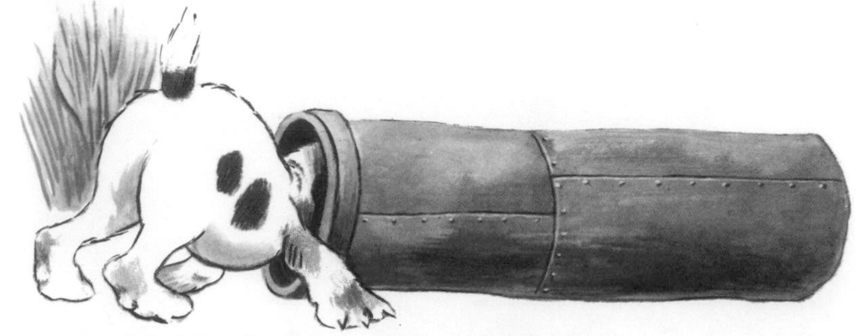

And he barked in a big round pipe.

And then one day he found an old oil drum.

He ran in that and barked, "Where's that big black dog now?"

And his bark sounded like this:

BOW WOW
WOW WOW
WOW WOW!!

The puppy liked that oil-drum bark. He practiced it every day—and every day his own little bark grew bigger and bigger. But he never noticed that.

The farmer didn't like all this noise.

"You're a fine watchdog, little puppy," he said. "But you'll have to use your own little bark after tomorrow, because I'm going to clean up the farm."

The next day while the farmer worked, the puppy ran at his heels.

"Oh, don't take my barrel!" he barked.

And he barked, "Don't take my oil-drum!"

And then he barked, "Don't take my milk can—or that old pipe. Oh, I need those old pails!"

But into the junk wagon they went.

"All my barking things are gone," cried the little puppy. "Now, what will I do when that big black dog comes back?"

And the very minute he said that, along came the big black dog! He walked boldly through the puppy's barnyard. He walked right up to the little puppy's house.

He licked up all the puppy's milk, and *then* he picked up the puppy's new chewing bone.

That was too much for the little puppy.

He ran at the big black dog like a small thunderbolt.

He was so angry that he barked for all he was worth, and by this time his own bark was a real big

BOW WOW WOW!

It was even bigger than his oil-drum bark!

The big dog never stopped to see how big the little

puppy was. He just dropped that bone and ran, with the puppy snapping at his tail. He jumped over the fence, he raced down the road, and he *never* came back.

Everybody on the farm came running out to see that chase.

"Just look at our watchdog!" squealed the pigs.

"And just listen to his bark!" the rooster crowed.

The farmer's wife was so pleased that she ran into the house for an old soft pillow. She put it in the doghouse.

"It will make a nice bed for our watchdog," she said.

The farmer filled the puppy's bowl with cream. He brought out a little dish of gravy with some fine juicy scraps of meat in it. He put a new chewing bone full of tid-bits beside the old chewing bone. And then he whistled a long, loud whistle for the little puppy.

When the little puppy got back to his house, he was the most surprised puppy in the whole world.

First, he barked a good-sized bark to say "Thank you,"

and then he began to eat. He ate until his little sides were as round as a pumpkin.

He tried out his lovely new bed.

It was so soft and comfortable that he almost fell asleep.

But he had one more thing to do.

The little puppy stood up on his four little feet and wagged his tail.

And just to make sure he was really a real watchdog, at last, he barked the loudest kind of bark—

BOW

WOW

WOW

THE COLOR KITTENS

BY MARGARET WISE BROWN • ILLUSTRATED BY ALICE AND MARTIN PROVENSEN

ONCE there were two color kittens with green eyes, Brush and Hush. They liked to mix and make colors by splashing one color into another. They had buckets and buckets and buckets and buckets of color to splash around with. Out of these colors they would make all the colors in the world.

The buckets had the colors written on them, but of course the kittens couldn't read. They had to tell by the colors. "It is very easy," said Brush.

"Red is red. Blue is blue," said Hush.

But they had no green. "No green paint!" said Brush and Hush. And they wanted green paint, of course, because nearly every place they liked to go was green.

Green as cats' eyes
Green as grass
By streams of water
Green as glass.

So they tried to make some green paint.

Brush mixed red paint and white paint together—and what did that make? It didn't make green.

But it made pink.
Pink as pigs
Pink as toes
Pink as a rose
Or a baby's nose.

Then Hush mixed yellow and red together,

and it made orange.

Orange as an orange tree
Orange as a bumblebee
Orange as the setting sun
Sinking slowly in the sea.

The kittens were delighted, but it didn't make green.

Then they mixed red and blue together—and what did that make? It didn't make green. It made a deep dark purple.

Purple as violets
Purple as prunes
Purple as shadows on late afternoons.

Still no green. And then . . .

O wonderful kittens! O Brush! O Hush!

At last, almost by accident, the kittens poured a bucket of blue and a bucket of yellow together, and it came to pass that they made a green as green as grass.

Green as green leaves on a tree
Green as islands in the sea.

The little kittens were so happy with all the colors they had made that they began to paint everything around them. They painted . . .

Green leaves
and red berries
and purple flowers
and pink cherries

Red tables and yellow chairs
Black trees with golden pears.

Then the kittens got so excited they knocked their buckets upside down and all the colors ran together. Yellow, red, a little blue and a little black . . . and that made brown.

Brown as a tugboat
Brown as an old goat
Brown as a beaver

And in all that brown, the sun went down. It was evening and the colors began to disappear in the warm dark night.

The kittens fell asleep in the warm dark night with all their colors out of sight and as they slept they dreamed their dream—

A wonderful dream
Of a red rose tree
That turned all white
When you counted three

One . . . Two . . . Three

Of a purple land
In a pale pink sea
Where apples fell
From a golden tree
And then a world of Easter eggs
That danced about on little short legs.
And they dreamed
Of a mouse
A little gray mouse
That danced on a cheese
That was big as a house
And a green cat danced
With a little pink dog
Till they all disappeared in a soft gray fog.

And suddenly Brush woke up and Hush woke up. It was morning. They crawled out of bed into a big bright world. The sky was wild with sunshine.

The kittens were wild
with purring
and pouncing—

They got so pouncy they knocked over the buckets and all the colors ran out together.

There were all the colors in the world and the color kittens had made them.

THE LITTLE FAT POLICEMAN

By Margaret Wise Brown
and Edith Thacher Hurd

Pictures by Alice and Martin Provensen

THE Little Fat Policeman stood in the middle of the street. He wore a new blue uniform with shiny buttons down the front. On his chest a silver badge said:

NO.9
POLICE
FORCE

The Little Fat Policeman directed all the whizzing traffic. He wore white gloves so that everyone could see his hands wave.

And he blew a silver whistle.

Everybody knew the Little Fat Policeman. When he blew his whistle the cars and trucks all stopped, until he waved his hand again for all the cars to go.

One day a lady with a bouncing baby in a carriage and six little funny-faced children wanted to cross the street.

The Little Fat Policeman blew his whistle extra hard and put up both his hands.

Everybody STOP!......

Then he wheeled the bouncing baby safe across the street. The lady thanked him. He saluted smartly. And all the funny-faced children smiled.

And he returned to his traffic, and there he stood.

Up came a red truck— STOP
Up came a blue car— STOP
Up came a yellow car— STOP
Up came a pink car and blew its horn— STOP
Up came a green car— STOP
Up came three jeeps— STOP
Up came a flower wagon— STOP
Up came a moving van— STOP
Up came a motorcycle— STOP
Up came a bicycle— STOP

Then the Little Fat Policeman gave them a look, raised his silver whistle to his mouth, and blew

Brr-rr went the red truck,
Brr-rr went the blue car,
Brr-rr went the yellow car,
Whump went the pink car,
Brr-rr went the green car,
Brr-rr-rr went the three jeeps,
Giddy ap! went the flower wagon,
Brr-rr went the moving van,
Brr-rr went the motorcycle,
and Whee went the bicycle.

GONE!......

The road was empty except for the Little Fat Policeman, who took off his hat and scratched his head.

Then way down the road he saw something coming fast—too fast. Zip—it grew bigger and bigger.

The Little Fat Policeman blew his whistle three times and waved his arms.

The car stopped and a lady leaned out and said, "Oh, dear! Oh, dear!"

"Too fast, lady!" said the Little Fat Policeman. "Why were you going so fast?"

"I was singing a very fast song and I forgot," said the lady. "I am very sorry."

"What were you singing?" asked the Little Fat Policeman.

"Glow, Little Glow Worm, Glimmer, Glimmer."

"Sing a slow song next time," said the Little Fat Policeman, "and don't forget or I'll have to give you a ticket and send you up before a judge."

Then he blew his whistle and waved her along. "Sing *Oh What a Beautiful Morning* next time," he called. And he started to hum it himself. Then down the road came—believe it or not—elephants, tigers in cages, clowns, monkeys, ladies on white horses, bears and peanuts.

The Circus had come to town.

So the Little Fat Policeman stopped all the cars at the crossroads and slowly but surely the circus went down the street.

A big parade!

With lions and tigers and a noisy brass band.

THE SUDDEN TELEPHONE CALL

BUT the Little Fat Policeman wasn't always just a traffic cop. Sometimes he waited in his Police Booth for exciting things to happen. One day a nice old lady called.

"Policeman, please!" said she. "I'm a Policeman," said he.

"Come quick as you can," said she.
"My cat is up in the top of a tree
And won't come down to me."
"I'll be right there," said he.
"Just sit in your chair
And I'll be right there."

The Little Fat Policeman put on his goggles, jumped on his red motorcycle, and stepped on the gas. He whizzed away.

"O, Little Fat Policeman, you've come just in time."

The old lady wrung her hands.

She mopped her eyes and began to jump about as if she had a fire inside her boots.

The Little Fat Policeman looked around but he couldn't see the cat until the old lady pointed to the top of a prickly pear tree—and THERE on top sat a cat!

The Little Fat Policeman didn't like to climb up prickly pear trees. He knew he was too fat, and he knew prickly pears were prickly. So he called the fire house.

The hook and ladder arrived in a jiffy. The firemen put a ladder up to the cat. And a fireman climbed up and brought the old lady's cat almost down, when—lickety split—the cat jumped out of his arms.

But the Little Fat Policeman jumped, as quick as lightning, after the cat.

He caught the cat in both his hands and gave it to the nice old lady. She hugged the cat and then she hugged the Little Fat Policeman. The cat was pushed between them. Meow! . . . . . .

THE BURGLAR IN THE DARK

ONE DARK night the Little Fat Policeman was waiting quietly at the Police Booth. He was all alone.

Br-rr-rr rang the telephone. Someone said, "Come fast, I think I hear a burglar prowling in my house."

The Little Fat Policeman stuck his pistol in his holster. He grabbed his stout policeman's billy.

Whee-ee-ee went the siren on the policeman's little car.

Then he turned the siren off and crept silently through the night. One Little Fat Policeman!

He crept up to the house. He walked on tiptoes, creeping, creeping. He flashed his flashlight all around.

He looked in the bushes and he looked in the trees.

He patted the pistol in the holster at his side. It was there, all right. He flashed his flashlight.

But there was no burglar there.

He went in the house. He crept in the hall.

Creeping, creeping, he flashed his flashlight.

But there was no burglar there.

He crept in the parlor. Creeping, creeping in the dark. He flashed his flashlight.

But there was no burglar there.

There was just a tiny little noise—a sort of scratching sound!

The Little Fat Policeman grabbed his pistol in his hand.

"Who's there?" he shouted softly.

The scratching stopped.

Instead there was a GROAN! and a SNEEZE!

The Little Fat Policeman pointed his pistol at the groan and the sneeze. Then he flashed his flashlight—FLASH!

And suddenly there was a lot of scrambling and a barking and a whining for joy.

Because that dreadful burglar was only a—BIG WOOLLY SHEEP DOG who had lost his way.

The Little Fat Policeman laughed a big fat belly laugh, a great big warm laugh. Then he patted the woolly sheep dog, who wagged his tail and licked the Little Fat Policeman's hand.

The Little Fat Policeman put him in his car and drove him home to the right house because he knew the boy who owned him.

THE BRAVE LIFE SAVER

EVERY Sunday morning the Little Fat Policeman took it easy. His wife shined his badge.

He liked to smoke his pipe and read his paper and take his wife out for a walk.

One Sunday the sun was shining brightly.

The birds were singing sweetly.

The Little Fat Policeman and his wife walked beside the ocean on the yellow sand. There were people lying on the beach. There were people swimming in the green sea. The Little Fat Policeman was eating a peach, when suddenly there was a dreadful yell:

"Help! Help! Help!"

The Little Fat Policeman saw a man who couldn't swim rolling in the waves.

As quick as a wink, before the man could sink, the Little Fat Policeman threw off his blue coat, kicked off his boots, threw down his cap, and ran. Down the beach he ran and took a dive into the waves.

And he dove and swam and kicked and splashed through the great, green, curling ocean.

The man kept bobbing up and down ahead of him and floating out to sea.

The Little Fat Policeman had learned how to rescue people when he went to policeman's school, so he knew what to do. He grabbed the man by the top of his head.

He pulled him by the hair, and swam with him up great, green waves, like mountains in the sea, until he swam safe back to shore.

The Little Fat Policeman's wife danced with joy. She danced upon the yellow sand. And all the people from the beach made a tremendous crowd. They shouted three hurrahs: "Hurrah!

Hurrah!

Hurrah!

For the Little Fat Policeman

The finest cop of all!"

And a little boy sang:

"Yo-ho-ho

Yes-sir-ree

O Policeman,

Please save me."

With stiff rhythm — *Music by Alec Wilder*

1. One Po - lice - man in the street, Blows his whis - tle, Tweet, tweet tweet! Some cars stop and some cars go — This Po - lice - man sig - nals GO.

Chorus

Yo ho ho! Yes sir - ee! O Po - lice - man, Please save me.

2. One Policeman all alone
In his round house
With his phone.
Ting-ling-ling
Rings in his ear—
This Policeman's always near.
Yo ho ho!
Yes siree!
O Policeman,
Please save me.

3. One Policeman on the beach
Keeps his feet dry,
Eats his peach.
Help! Help! Help!
Now don't you fear—
This Policeman's always near.
Yo ho ho!
Yes siree!
O Policeman,
Please save me.

BY KATHRYN JACKSON

PICTURES BY LEONARD WEISGARD

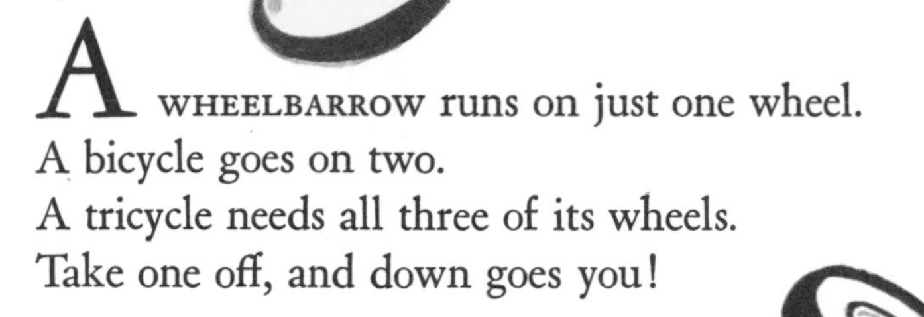

A WHEELBARROW runs on just one wheel.
A bicycle goes on two.
A tricycle needs all three of its wheels.
Take one off, and down goes you!

A car has two big wheels in front
and two big wheels in back,
and a spare in case one goes flat,
and a steering wheel for steering with,
and a horn that goes beep! like that.

There are four wheels each on roller skates.
"Come on, let's have a race!"
And the clock has dozens of busy wheels
in back of its quiet face.

A motorcycle has two swift wheels,
and sometimes a seat on the side.
"Hop in, hold tight and hold your hat—
I'll take you for a ride!"

Some wheels go up.
Some wheels go down.
The clothesline goes around.
"I'll make it roll—
you hang the clothes—
don't let them touch the ground!"

A tractor has a steering wheel
and four big wheels that run.
The lawnmower wheels turn its cutting blades
and all sparkly in the sun
is the water on the big boat wheels
as they go splashing round.

A water wheel runs the old stone mill
where pancake flour is ground.
And next comes a wheel
that's a sideways wheel.
Of course, it's a merry-go-round!

The grocery cart has four low wheels.
A ride in it is lots of fun!
And the trolley car has one high-up wheel.
That's the one that makes it run.

A truck has double wheels in back—
a big bus has them, too.
But the fastest wheels are the eight red wheels
on the hook and ladder—whoooo!

The ferris wheel is the biggest wheel
that ever was anywhere.
It takes you up, and up, and up
for a ride high in the air!

And when you're in bed, a silvery wheel
rolls slowly across the sky, while all sorts
of wheels go by in the dark.
You can hear them if you try.

TAWNY SCRAWNY LION

BY KATHRYN JACKSON

PICTURES BY GUSTAF TENGGREN

ONCE there was a tawny, scrawny, hungry lion who never could get enough to eat.

He chased monkeys on Monday—kangaroos on Tuesday—zebras on Wednesday—bears on Thursday—camels on Friday—and on Saturday, elephants!

And since he caught everything he ran after, that lion should have been as fat as butter. But he wasn't at all. The more he ate, the scrawnier and hungrier he grew.

The other animals didn't feel one bit safe. They stood at a distance and tried to talk things over with the tawny, scrawny lion.

"It's all your fault for running away," he grumbled. "If I didn't have to run, run, run for every single bite I get, I'd be fat as butter and sleek as satin. Then I wouldn't have to eat so much, and you'd last longer!"

Just then, a fat little rabbit came hopping through the forest, picking berries. All the big animals looked at him and grinned slyly.

"Rabbit," they said. "Oh, you lucky rabbit! We appoint you to talk things over with the lion."

That made the little rabbit feel very proud.

"What shall I talk about?" he asked eagerly.

"Any old thing," said the big animals. "The important thing is to go right up close."

So the fat little rabbit hopped right up to the big hungry lion and counted his ribs.

"You look much too scrawny to talk things over," he said. "So how about supper at my house first?"

"What's for supper?" asked the lion.

The little rabbit said, "Carrot stew." That sounded awful to the lion. But the little rabbit said, "Yes sir, my five fat sisters and my four fat brothers are making a delicious big carrot stew right now!"

"What are we waiting for?" cried the lion. And he went hopping away with the little rabbit, thinking of ten fat rabbits, and looking just as jolly as you please.

"Well," grinned all the big animals. "That should take care of Tawny-Scrawny for today."

Before very long, the lion began to wonder if they would ever get to the rabbit's house.

First, the fat little rabbit kept stopping to pick berries and mushrooms and all sorts of good-smelling herbs. And when his basket was full, what did he do but flop down on the river bank!

"Wait a bit," he said. "I want to catch a few fish for the stew."

That was almost too much for the hungry lion.

For a moment, he thought he would have to eat that one little rabbit then and there. But he kept saying, "five fat sisters and four fat brothers" over and over to himself. And at last the two were on their way again.

"Here we are!" said the rabbit, hopping around a turn with the lion close behind him. Sure enough, there was the rabbit's house, with a big pot of carrot stew bubbling over an open fire.

And sure enough, there were nine more fat, merry little rabbits hopping around it!

When they saw the fish, they popped them into the stew, along with the mushrooms and herbs. The stew began to smell very good indeed.

And when they saw the tawny, scrawny lion, they gave him a big bowl of hot stew. And then they hopped about so busily, that really, it would have been quite a job for that tired, hungry lion to catch even one of them!

So he gobbled his stew, but the rabbits filled his bowl again. When he had eaten all he could hold, they heaped his bowl with berries.

And when the berries were gone—the tawny, scrawny lion wasn't scrawny any more! He felt so good and fat and comfortable that he couldn't even move.

"Here's a fine thing!" he said to himself. "All these fat little rabbits, and I haven't room inside for even one!"

He looked at all those fine, fat little rabbits and wished he'd get hungry again.

"Mind if I stay a while?" he asked.

"We wouldn't even hear of your going!" said the rabbits. Then they plumped themselves down in the lion's lap and began to sing songs.

And somehow, even when it was time to say goodnight, that lion wasn't one bit hungry!

Home he went, through the soft moonlight, singing softly to himself. He curled up in his bed, patted his sleek, fat tummy, and smiled.

When he woke up in the morning, it was Monday.

"Time to chase monkeys!" said the lion.

But he wasn't one bit hungry for monkeys! What he wanted was some more of that tasty carrot stew. So off he went to visit the rabbits.

On Tuesday he didn't want kangaroos, and on Wednesday he didn't want zebras. He wasn't hungry for bears on Thursday, or camels on Friday, or elephants on Saturday.

All the big animals were so surprised and happy!

They dressed in their best and went to see the fat little rabbit.

"Rabbit," they said. "Oh, you wonderful rabbit! What in the world did you talk to the tawny, scrawny, hungry, terrible lion about?"

The fat little rabbit jumped up in the air and said, "Oh, my goodness! We had such a good time with that nice, jolly lion that I guess we forgot to talk about anything at all!"

And before the big animals could say one word, the tawny lion came skipping up the path. He had a basket of berries for the fat rabbit sisters, and a string of fish for the fat rabbit brothers, and a big bunch of daisies for the fat rabbit himself.

"I came for supper," he said, shaking paws all around.

Then he sat down in the soft grass, looking fat as butter, sleek as satin, and jolly as all get out, all ready for another good big supper of carrot stew.

THE TRAIN TO TIMBUCTOO

BY MARGARET WISE BROWN

PICTURES BY ART SEIDEN

Clackety clack—clackety clack
There was a big train
and clickety click—clickety click—clickety click
There was a very little train.

They were on their way
home to Timbuctoo.
And they had just left
the town of Kalamazoo.

Slam Bang grease the engine
throw out the throttle and give it the gun.
There was a big engineer
who drove the big engine.
And Slam Bang grease the engine
throw out the throttle and give it the gun.
There was a little engineer
who drove the little engine.
When the big engine went through a tunnel
The big engineer blew his big whistle
whooooooooooooooooooooooooooo
When the little engine went through a tunnel
The little engineer blew his whistle
wheeeeeeeeeeeeeeeeeeeeeeeeeeeeeeeeeeeeeeeeeeeeeee
And clackety clack—clickety click
Throw out the throttle and give it the gun
whoooooooooooooooooooooooooo
wheeeeeeeeeeeeeeeeeeeeeeeeeeeeeeeeeeeeeeeeeeeeeeeeee
Out from the big tunnel came the big engine
With the big engineer
And the big coal car
And the big baggage car
And the big passenger car
And the big dining car and the big
sleeping car and the little caboose
And then out from the little tunnel
Came the little engine
With the little engineer
And a little coal car
And the little baggage car
And the little passenger car

And the little dining car
And the little sleeping car
And a little caboose
Clickety click—clickety click
clackety clack—clackety clack
whoooooooooooooooooooooooooooooo
wheeeeeeeeeeeeeeeeeeeeeeeeeeeeeeeeeeeeeeeeeeeeee
That great big train and that little tiny train
went roaring by.

Then clackety clack—
clackety clack
The big train came
to a big bridge over a big river
And over the big bridge
went the big engine
With
The big engineer
And the big coal car
And the big baggage car
And the big passenger car
And the big dining car

And the big sleeping car
And the little caboose
Then
Clickety click—clickety click
The little train came to a little bridge
Over a river, over a little river,

And clickety click—clickety click
Over the little bridge went the little engine
With the little engineer
And the little coal car
And the little baggage car
And the little passenger car
And the little dining car
And the little sleeping car
And the little caboose
And clickety click—clickety click
clackety clack—clackety clack—
pocketa—pocketa—pocketa—pocketa
pocketa—pocketa—pocketa—pocketa
The trains rolled on towards Timbuctoo
Far down the track from Kalamazoo
Until far away against the sky
There was a great big railroad station
And far away against the sky
There was a little railroad station.
whoooooooooo
wheeeeeeeeeeeeeeeeee
As ringing their bells
dong—dong—dong
ding—ding—ding
That great big train with a puff—puff—puff
And that tiny little train
with a puff—puff—puff
Came home to Timbuctoo.
And if you switch
the names of the towns
in the front of the book
You can get back to
Kalamazoo.

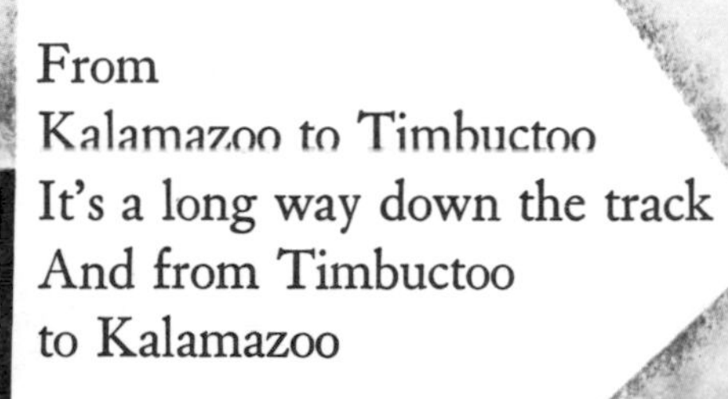

From
Kalamazoo to Timbuctoo
It's a long way down the track
And from Timbuctoo
to Kalamazoo

It's just as far to go back
From Timbuctoo to Kalamazoo
From Kalamazoo and back
A long, long way,
A long, long way,
a long way down the track.
From Kalamazoo to Timbuctoo
From Timbuctoo
and back.

LITTLE BOY WITH A BIG HORN

BY JACK BECHDOLT
PICTURES BY
AURELIUS BATTAGLIA

OLLIE was learning to play the bass horn. Ollie was a small boy. And the horn was a big horn.

He knew only one tune. It was called "Asleep in the Deep." It told about a shipwreck and brave sailors.

Maybe you know that tune.

The music goes way down deep, like this:

"MANY BRAVE HEARTS
ARE ASLEEP IN THE DEEP SO BEWARE
BEEEEE
E
E
E
WARE!"

Ollie loved that song, but . . .

Ollie's mother said, "Please, NOT in the house, Ollie. I can't think straight about my housework."

"Yes, Mother," said Ollie and took his horn into the back yard.

"Beeeeee-ware . . . BEEEE-WARE!" boomed the big horn.

"Owroooo!" howled all the town dogs.

"Oh bother!" said all the neighbors.

"MANY
BRAVE HEARTS
ARE ASLEEP IN
THE DEEP SO BEWARE
BEEEEEE
E
E
E
WARE!"

The Grocer dropped a crate of eggs.

The Preacher couldn't write his sermon.

The Farmer's horses ran away.

Everybody agreed that the town must do something to stop Ollie from playing that horn.

All together they called on Ollie's mother.

"We love music," they said, "but too much is TOO MUCH!"

"But the boy must practice," said Ollie's mother.

"Perhaps, but not here," said the neighbors.

"We must think of a better place," said Ollie's mother.

"Yes, yes, a better place," they all agreed. "But where?"

Everyone thought hard.

"I have it," Ollie cried.

Everybody stopped thinking and looked at him.

"I'll go way off in the fields. Nobody can hear me there."

"Splendid!" said everybody.

"Wonderful idea!" they agreed.
"Ollie is a good boy," said his proud mother.
Ollie set out for the distant pastures.
The sun was hot.
He grew tired. But he kept on.
Far from home, he stopped at last.
He spread out his music and took up his horn.
First he played, "Unk . . . unk . . . UNK."
Then he played "Asleep in the Deep."
Surely nobody would mind now, for there was nobody to mind!
But somebody did mind!
Over the hill the Farmer's cows were grazing.
"Beeeeee-WARE!" boomed the big horn.
The cattle raised their heads.
They had never heard the like of it. They began to gather from near and far. They began to move toward the strange noise.
"Moo!" said one.
"Arooo!" bawled another.
The busy Farmer heard them.
"Drat," he said. "The old muley has fallen into the ditch again."
Pitchfork in hand, he came running to rescue his cows.

When he saw Ollie, the Farmer was angry.
"You can't play that horn here," he said. "It's enough to sour their milk."
"Oh, dear," sighed Ollie.
He picked up his horn and turned homeward.
The sun shone hot on his back.
He was thirsty. And tired.

"Seems as if there is no place in the world where I can learn to play my horn," he sighed.
And then he had another bright idea.

Far off he saw the ocean.

"I'll go down to the ocean," said Ollie. "There's nobody there but fish and seagulls, and they won't mind my music."

So he went and got his rowboat and began to row far out from the shore.

He played "Asleep in the Deep," because that was the only tune he knew.

A big gray gull circled over his head. Then another. And another.

"Awk-awk-awk-awk," they shouted angrily.

Some dangerous rocks marked the entrance to the harbor.

The rocks were guarded by a bell buoy that tolled a warning to incoming vessels.

But when Ollie reached the rocks the bell buoy was not there. It had drifted away.

There was nothing to warn the vessels.

And now a thick fog was spreading over the ocean.

It shut out sight of everything, even the rocks near by.

Every day at this time a steamship brought passengers and freight to the town where Ollie lived.

The ship must be somewhere near even now, lost in the fog.

There was no warning bell to tell its captain when he was near the rocks.

The ship might strike on the reef.

"I'll stay here and play on my horn," Ollie decided. "That will be a warning."

So Ollie stayed. And he played.

Some seals that lived on the rocks began to bark a protest, "Owk-owk-owk!"

"I am very sorry if you don't like my music," said Ollie politely, "but I'm NOT going away."

He kept right on playing to warn the lost ship of her danger.

The ship was drawing closer.

The captain peered through the fog.

He and his crew could see nothing.

They listened for the bell buoy's warning.

They could hear nothing but the sea.

But what was that noise?

"Bee-WARE!" boomed Ollie's big horn.

The men on the ship were amazed.

"Stop the ship," cried the Captain. "Lower a boat and find out what's making music out here on the ocean."

And that was how they found Ollie and escaped being wrecked upon the rocks.

"We owe our lives to this brave boy," said the steamship Captain.

All the passengers cheered.

When the ship reached her dock all the town heard of Ollie's brave deed.

"He must be rewarded," they said.

And a big public meeting was held at the Town Hall.

The Mayor gave Ollie a handsome medal marked

"FOR BRAVERY"

and said the town would send Ollie to music school.

Ollie thanked the Mayor.

"I will be able to play my horn as much as I like," he said. "And the school is so far from our town that nobody will be disturbed any more."

Everybody cheered and said that Ollie was as wise as he was brave.

SEVEN LITTLE POSTMEN

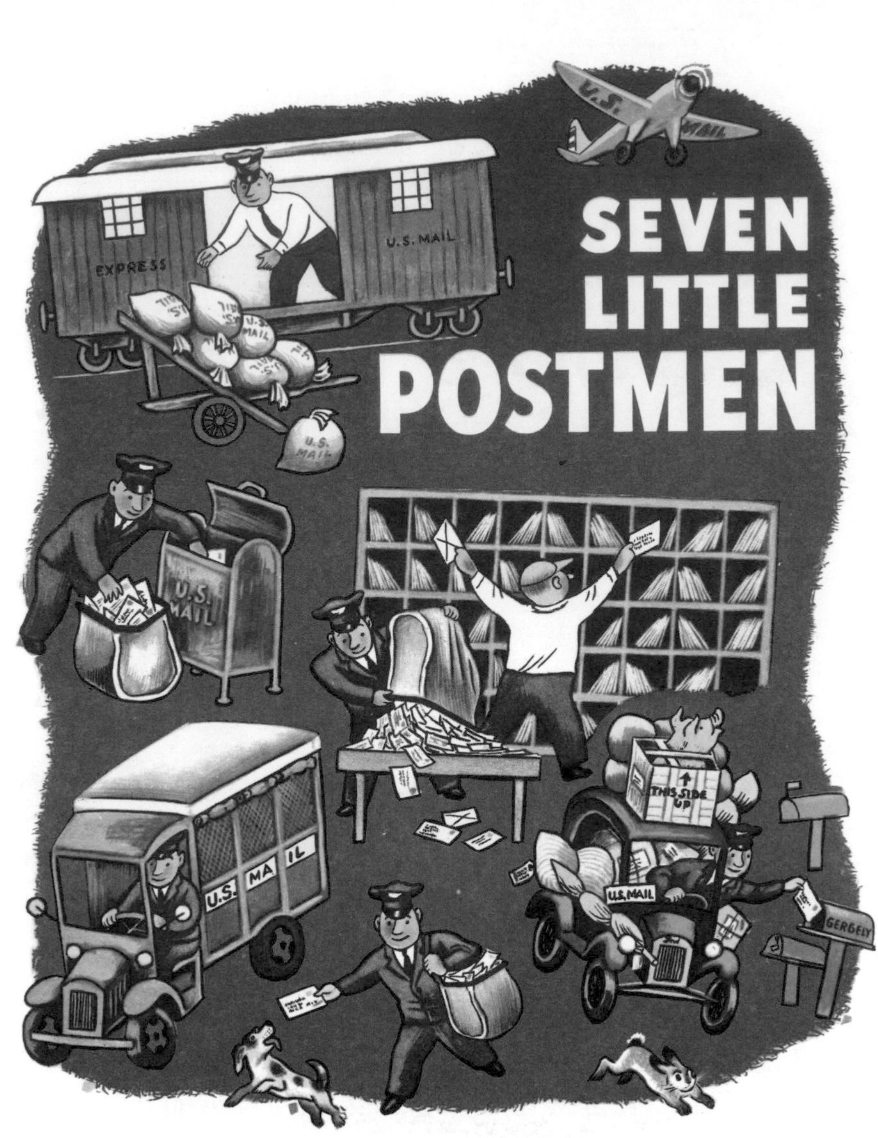

BY MARGARET WISE BROWN
AND EDITH THACHER HURD

A BOY had a secret. It was a surprise.
He wanted to tell his grandmother.
So he sent his secret through the mail.
The story of that letter
Is the reason for this tale
Of the seven little postmen who carried the mail.
Because there was a secret in the letter
The boy sealed it with red sealing wax.
If anyone broke the seal
The secret would be out.
He slipped the letter into the mail box.
The first little postman
Took it from the box,
Put it in his bag,
And walked seventeen blocks
To a big Post Office
All built of rocks.
The letter with the secret
Was dumped on a table
With big and small letters
That all needed the label
Of the big Post Office.
Stamp stamp, clickety click,
The machinery ran with a quick sharp tick.
The letter with the secret is stamped at last
And the round black circle tells that it passed

Through the cancelling machine
  Whizz whizz fast!
Big letters
Small letters
Thin and tall—
The second little postman
Sorts them all.
The letters are sorted

From East to West
From North to South.
"And this letter
Had best go West,"
Said the second
Little postman,
Scratching his chest.
Into the pouch
Lock it tight
The secret letter
Must travel all night. 
The third little postman in the big mail car
Comes to a crossroad where waiting are
A green, a yellow, and a purple car.
They all stop there. There is nothing to say.
The mail truck has the right of way!
"The mail must go through!"
Up and away through sleet and hail
This airplane carries the fastest mail.
The pilot flies through whirling snow
As far and as fast as the plane can go.
And he drops the mail for the evening train.
Now hang the pouch on the big hook crane!
The engine speeds up the shining rails
  And the fourth little postman
  Grabs the mails with a giant hook.

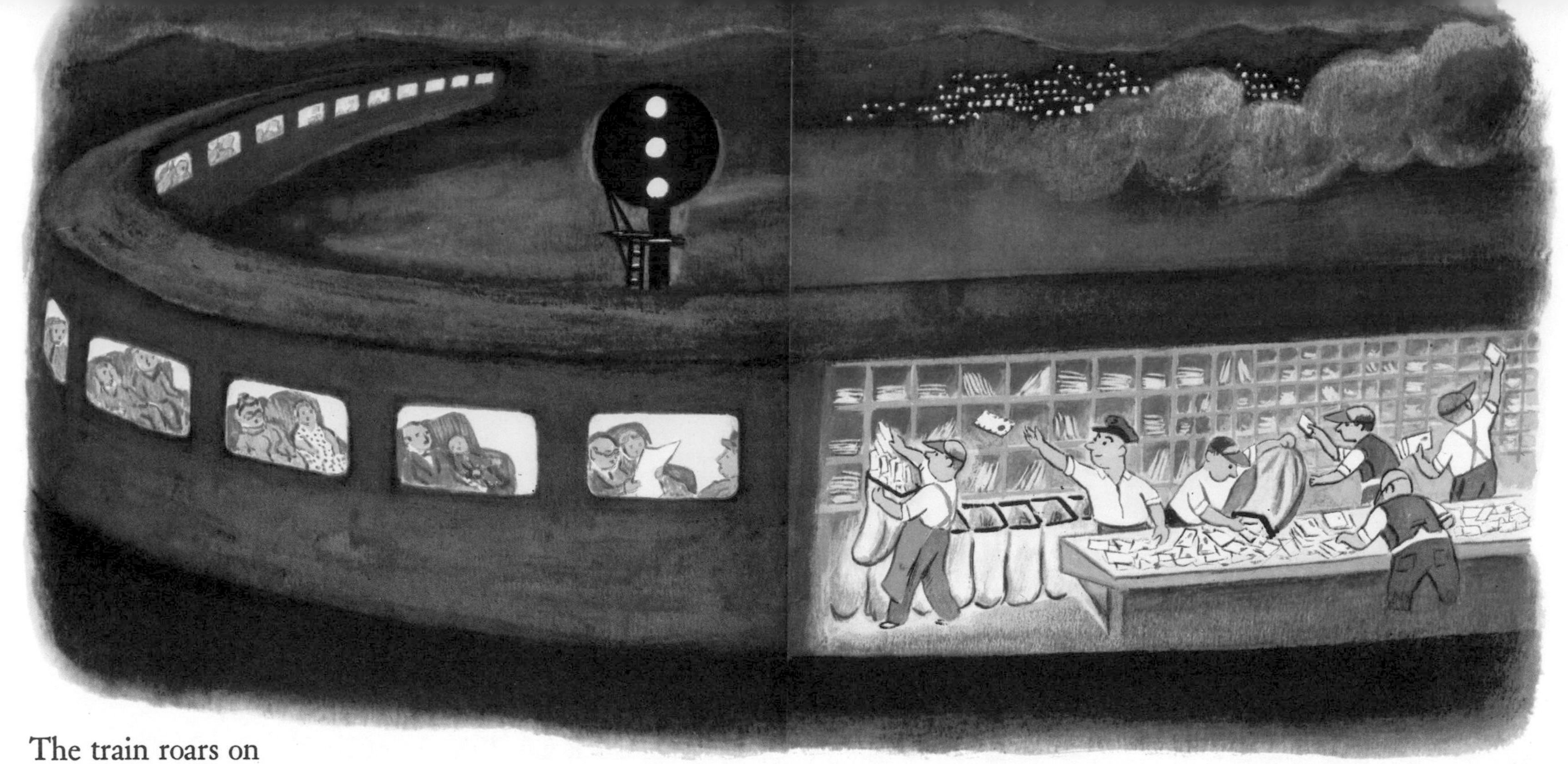

The train roars on
With a puff and a snort
And the fourth little postman
Begins to sort.
The train carries the letter
Through gloom of night
In a mail car filled with electric light
To a country postman
By a country road
Where the fifth little postman
Is waiting for his load.

The mail clerk
Heaves the mail pouch
With all his might
To the fifth little postman
Who grabs it tight.

Then off he goes
Along the lane
And over the hill
Until

He comes to a little town
That is very small—
So very small
The Post Office there
Is hardly one at all.
The sixth little postman
In great big boots
Sorts the letters
For their various routes—
Some down the river,
Some over the hill.
But the secret letter
Goes farther still.

The seventh little postman on R.F.D.
Carries letters and papers, chickens and fruit
To the people who live along his route.
He stops to deliver some sugar
To Mr. Jones who keeps a store
And always seems to need something more.
For Mrs. O'Finnigan with all her ills
He brings a bottle of bright pink pills,
And an airmail letter that cost seven cents
He hands to a farmer over the fence.
There were parts for a tractor
And a wig for an actor
And a funny post card for a little boy

Playing in his own backyard.
There was something for Sally

And something for Sam
And something for Mrs. Potter
Who was busy making jam.

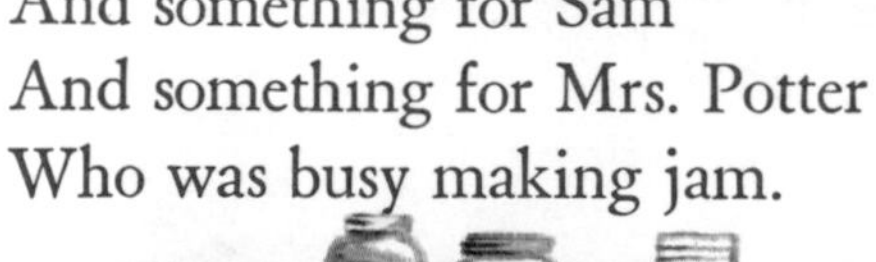

There were dozens of chickens for Mrs. Pickens
And a dress for a party for Mrs. McCarty.
There was a special delivery—crisp orange and blue.
What was the hurry, nobody knew.

At the last house along the way sat the grandmother of the boy who had sent the letter with the secret in it. She had been wishing all day he would come to visit. For she lived all alone in a tiny house and was sometimes lonely.

The Postman blew his whistle and gave her the letter with the red sealing wax on it—the secret letter!

"Sakes alive! What is it about?" Sakes Alive!

The secret is out! What does it say?

DEAREST GRANNY:
I AM WRITING TO SAY
THAT I'M COMING TO VISIT ON SATURDAY.
MY CAT HAS SEVEN KITTENS AND I AM BRINGING
ONE TO YOU FOR YOUR VERY OWN KITTEN.
THE POSTMAN IS MY FRIEND.
YOUR GRANDSON
THOMAS

SEVEN LITTLE POSTMEN

Seven Little Postmen carried the mail
Through Rain and Snow and Wind and Hail
Through Snow and Rain and Gloom of Night

Seven Little Postmen
Out of sight.
Over Land and Sea
Through Air and Light
Through Snow and Rain
And Gloom of Night—
Put a stamp on your letter
And seal it tight.

MISTER DOG
The Dog Who Belonged to Himself

BY MARGARET WISE BROWN

PICTURES BY GARTH WILLIAMS

ONCE upon a time there was a funny dog named Crispin's Crispian. He was named Crispin's Crispian because—
he belonged to himself.

In the mornings he woke himself up and he went to the icebox and gave himself some bread and milk. He was a funny old dog. He liked strawberries.

Then he took himself for a walk. And he went wherever he wanted to go.

But one morning he didn't know where he wanted to go.

"Just walk and sooner or later you'll get somewhere," he said to himself.

Soon he came to a country where there were lots of dogs. They barked at him and he barked back. Then they all played together.

But he still wanted to go somewhere so he walked on until he came to a country where there were lots of cats and rabbits.

The cats and rabbits jumped in the air and ran. So Crispian jumped in the air and ran after them.

He didn't catch them because he ran bang into a little boy.

"Who are you and who do you belong to?" asked the little boy.

"I am Crispin's Crispian and I belong to myself," said Crispian. "Who and what are you?"

"I am a boy," said the boy, "and I belong to myself."

"I am so glad," said Crispin's Crispian. "Come and live with me."

So the boy walked on with Crispian and threw him sticks to chase, all through the shining, sun-drenched morning.

"I'm hungry," said Crispin's Crispian.

"I'm hungry, too," said the boy's little boy.

So they went to a butcher shop—"to get his poor dog a bone," Crispian said.

Now since Crispin's Crispian belonged to himself, he gave himself the bone and trotted home with it.

And the boy bought a big lamb chop and a bright green vegetable and trotted home with Crispin's Crispian.

Crispin's Crispian lived in two-story doghouse in a garden.

And in his two-story doghouse he had a little fur living room with a warm fire that crackled all winter and went out in the summer.

His house was always warm. His house had a chimney for the smoke to go out.

And there was plenty of room in his house for the boy to live there with him.

Crispian went upstairs, and the boy went with him.

And upstairs he had a little bedroom with a bed in it

and a place for his leash and a pillow under which he hid his bones.

And he had windows to look out of and a garden to run around in any time he felt like running around in it. The garden was blooming with dogwood and dogtooth violets.

And he had a little kitchen upstairs in his two-story doghouse where he fixed himself a good dinner three times a day because he liked to eat. He liked steaks and chops and roast beef and chopped meat and raw eggs.

This evening he made a bone soup with lots of meat in it. He gave some to the boy and the boy liked it. The boy didn't give Crispian his chop bone but he put some of his bright green vegetables in the soup.

And what did Crispian do with his dinner?

Did he put it in his stomach?

Yes, indeed.

He chewed it up and swallowed it into his little fat stomach.

And what did the little boy do with his dinner?

Did he put it in his stomach?

Yes, indeed.

He chewed it up and swallowed it into his little fat stomach.

Crispin's Crispian was a *conservative*. He liked everything at the right time—

dinner at dinnertime,
lunch at lunchtime,
breakfast in time for breakfast,
and sunrise at sunrise,
and sunset at sunset.
And at bedtime—

At bedtime he liked everything in its own place—

the cup in the saucer,
the chair under the table,
the stars in the heavens,
the moon in the sky,
and himself in his own little bed.

And then what did he do?

Then he curled in a warm little heap and went to sleep. And he dreamed his own dreams.

That was what the dog who belonged to himself did.

And what did the boy who belonged to himself do? The boy who belonged to himself curled in a warm little heap and went to sleep. And he dreamed his own dreams.

That was what the boy who belonged to himself did.

THE HAPPY MAN AND HIS DUMP TRUCK

BY MIRYAM

PICTURES BY TIBOR GERGELY

ONCE upon a time there was a man who had a dump truck.

Every time he saw a friend, he would wave his hand and tip the dumper.

One day he was riding in his dump truck, singing a happy song, when he met a pig going along the road.

"Would you like a ride in my dump truck?" he asked.

"Oh, thank you!" said the pig. And he climbed into the back of the truck.

After they had gone a little way down the road, the man saw a friend.

He waved his hand merrily and tipped the dumper.

"Whee," said the pig. "What fun!" And he slid all the way down to the bottom of the dumper.

Very soon they came to a farm.

"Here is where my friends live," said the pig. "You have a nice dump truck.

"Would you please let my friends see your truck?"

"I will give them a ride in my dump truck," said the man.

So the hen and the rooster climbed into the truck.

And the duck climbed into the truck.

And the dog and the cat climbed into the truck.

And the pig climbed back into the truck, too.

And the man closed the tail gate, so they would not fall out.

And then off they went!

They went past the farm, and all the animals waved to the farmer.

The man was very happy. "They are all my friends," he said.

So he waved his hand, and tipped the dumper.

The hen, the rooster, the duck, the dog, the cat, and the pig all slid down the dumper into a big heap!

The hen clucked.

The duck quacked.

The rooster crowed.

The dog barked.

The cat mewed.

And the pig said a great big grunt.

The animals were all so happy!

Then the man took them for a long ride, and drove them back to the farm.

He opened the tail gate wide and raised the dumper all the way up.

All the animals slid off the truck onto the ground.

"What a fine sliding-board," they all said.

"Thank you," said all the animals.

"Cut, cut,"
clucked the hen.

"Cock-a-doodle-doo,"
the rooster crowed.

"Quack, quack,"
quacked the duck.

"Bow-wow,"
barked the dog.

"Meow, meow,"
mewed the cat.

And the pig said a great big grunt.

"Oink, oink!"

The man waved his hand and tipped the dumper, and he rode off in his dump truck, singing a happy song.

Four Little Kittens

BY KATHLEEN N. DALY

PICTURES BY

ADRIANA MAZZA SAVIOZZI

Once upon a time, four kittens were born in a corner of a barn.

"I wonder what kind of cats they'll grow up to be," thought the mother cat.

She licked her four new babies proudly. They were still tiny. Their eyes were sealed shut, and they could only mew, and snuggle close to their mother's warm side.

In a few days, the kittens opened their eyes. Each day they grew a little bigger, and a little stronger. "And a great deal naughtier," thought Mother Cat, as they pounced on her twitchy tail.

"Children," she said one day, "the time has come for you to decide what kind of cats you will be."

"Tell us, tell us," mewed the kittens, "what kind of cats there are."

Mother Cat sat up straight, and half closed her green eyes, and began.

"There are Alley Cats.

"An Alley Cat is long and lean. He slinks like a shadow, sleeps where he can, eats what he finds.

"A free cat is he—no manners to mind, no washing of paws, no sheathing of claws. He does what he likes, and nobody knows but he.

"Your Uncle Tom is an Alley Cat. Many friends he has, and they make fine music at night, to the moon. His enemies are stray dogs, and turning wheels, and cold, sleety rain. He's a wild and clever cat, the Alley Cat."

"That is the life for me," said Tuff, the biggest kitten. And off he went, to be an Alley Cat, like bold Uncle Tom.

"Now Uncle Tar was a Ship's Cat," Mother Cat went on. "A splendid cat he was, with a ship for a home, and sailors for friends.

"A Ship's Cat visits seaports a thousand miles away, and talks to foreign cats, and chases foreign rats that try to come aboard.

"A brave cat is he, a jolly, roving cat, a Ship's Cat. And many are the tales your Uncle Tar could tell."

"That is the life for me," said Luff, the second kitten. And off he went, to be a Ship's Cat, like jolly Uncle Tar.

"And," said Mother Cat, "there are Farm Cats.

"I am a Farm Cat, a useful cat. I catch the mice and chase the rats, while the farmer sleeps at night.

"I live in the barn on a bed of straw—no House Cat am I.

"A Farm Cat can talk to all the animals that live on the farm. A splendid, useful, strong cat is the Farm Cat—though I say it myself."

"That is the life for me," said Ruff, the third kitten. And off he went, to be a Farm Cat, like his mother. Mother Cat purred.

Now the smallest, youngest kitten was called Muff. Muff was gentle, and playful, and pretty, and always kept her white paws clean.

Muff's mother sighed and said, "Muff, I don't think you are an Alley Cat. I don't think you are a Ship's Cat, or even a Farm Cat. I don't know what kind of cat you are."

And off went Mother Cat, to catch a nice, fat mouse for dinner.

Sadly, Muff wandered out of the barn.

She caught sight of Ruff, getting ready to spring on a

great big rat. Muff shivered, and crept by as quietly as she could.

"I couldn't be a Farm Cat," said Muff, "because I'm *afraid* of big rats."

Muff wandered out of the farm and down to the village.

She saw plump little Tuff, doing his best to look lean and wild like an Alley Cat.

"Wuff, wuff," barked a little stray dog, and Tuff arched his back, and bristled his fur, and spat and hissed in his best Alley Cat way.

The little dog ran away. And so did Muff.

Down to the river she ran, and she saw Luff on a big ship in the harbor.

The sailors were busy with ropes and things, but already Luff had curled up in a place where he wouldn't be in the way. Soon Luff would be visiting cats a thousand miles away, just like Uncle Tar.

Muff waved good-by. "I wish I knew what kind of cat *I* am," she sighed. Then she had to run out of the way as a bicycle came by.

It began to rain, and Muff got cold and wet. She didn't like that at all, and she shook her wet paws crossly. She lay down to sleep on a lumpy pile of sacks. She didn't like that very much, either.

She was cold and hungry and cross, and when a big hand picked her up, she spat and hissed for all the world like an Alley Cat.

But the big hand put her into a big, warm pocket, and after a few more angry squawks, and a sad little mew, Muff fell asleep.

When next she opened her eyes, Muff was in a house. There were cushions and carpets and curtains. There was a warm, crackling fire.

There was a little girl with soft, gentle hands.

"Oh, what a lovely kitten," said the little girl. "Oh, I wanted a kitten so much. Now I won't be lonely any more."

The little girl gave Muff a saucer of cream.

Muff drank it all, with one white foot in the saucer to keep it steady. Then she washed her paw, and licked her whiskers.

This was *much* better than fat mice for dinner.

The little girl played with Muff. She dangled a string, and Muff jumped and pounced in her prettiest way, and the little girl laughed with delight.

Muff purred.

This was much better than running away from barking dogs, and turning wheels.

The little girl lifted Muff onto her warm lap, and stroked Muff's fur.

"Oh, it's nice to have a kitten," said the little girl.

Muff purred loudly.

This was much better than a pile of lumpy sacks, or even a bed of straw.

"This is the life for me," purred Muff. "I know what kind of cat I am. I'm a cushion and cream cat, a purring cat, a cuddlesome cat, a playful cat, a little girl's cat—I'm a House Cat!"

And so all four kittens lived happily ever after—Tuff in his alley, because he was an Alley Cat, Ruff on his farm, because he was a Farm Cat, Luff on his ship, because he was a Ship's Cat, and Muff on her cushions, in her house, with her little girl, because she was a House Cat.

Born at sea in the teeth of a gale, the sailor was a dog. Scuppers was his name.

After that he lived on a farm. But Scuppers, born at sea, was a sailor. And when he grew up he wanted to go to sea.

So he went to look for something to go in.

He found a big airplane. "All aboard!" they called. It was going up in the sky. But Scuppers did not want to go up in the sky.

He found a little submarine. "All aboard!" they called. It was going down under the sea. But Scuppers did not want to go under the sea.

He found a little car.

"All aboard!" they called. It was going over the land. But Scuppers did not want to go over the land.

He found a subway train.

"All aboard!" they called. It was going under the earth. But Scuppers did not want to go under the earth.

Scuppers was a sailor. He wanted to go to sea.

So Scuppers went over the hills and far away until he came to the sea.

Over the hills and far away was the ocean. And on the ocean was a ship. The ship was about to go over the sea. It blew all its whistles.

"All aboard!" they called.

"All ashore that are going ashore!"

"All aboard!"

So Scuppers went to sea.

The ship began to move slowly along. The wind blew it.

In his ship Scuppers had a little room. In his room Scuppers had a hook for his hat and a hook for his rope and a hook for his handkerchief and a hook for his pants and a hook for his spyglass and a place for his shoes and a bunk for a bed to put himself in.

At night Scuppers threw the anchor into the sea and he went down to his little room.

He put his hat on the hook for his hat, and his rope on the hook for his rope, and his pants on the hook for his pants, and his spyglass on the hook for his spyglass, and he put his shoes under the bed, and got into his bed, which was a bunk, and went to sleep.

Next morning he was shipwrecked.

Too big a storm blew out of the sky. The anchor dragged and the ship crashed onto the rocks. There was a big hole in it.

Scuppers himself was washed overboard and hurled by huge waves onto the shore.

He was washed up onto the beach. It was foggy and rainy. There were no houses and Scuppers needed a house.

But on the beach was lots and lots of driftwood, and he found an old rusty box stuck in the sand.

Maybe it was a treasure!

It was a treasure—to Scuppers.

It was an old-fashioned tool box with hammers and nails and an ax and a saw. Everything he needed to build himself a house. So Scuppers started to build a house, all by himself, out of driftwood.

He built a door and a window and a roof and a porch and a floor, all out of driftwood.

And he found some red bricks and built a big red chimney. And then he lit a fire and the smoke went up the chimney.

After building his house he was hungry. So he went fishing. He went fishing in a big river. The first fish he caught never came up. The second fish he caught got away. The third fish he caught was too little, but the next fish he caught was—just right.

Now he is cooking the fish he caught in the house he built, and smoke is going up the chimney.

Then the stars came out and he was sleepy. So he built a bed of pine branches.

And he jumped into his deep green bed and went to sleep. As he slept he dreamed—

If he could build a house
he could mend the hole in the ship.

So the next day at low tide he took his tool box and waded out and hammered planks across the hole in his ship.

At last the ship was fixed.

So he sailed away.

Until he came to a seaport in a foreign land.

By now his clothes were all worn and ripped and torn and blown to pieces. His coat was torn, his hat was blown away, and his shoes were all worn out. And his handkerchief was ripped. Only his pants were still good.

So he went ashore to buy some clothes at the Army and Navy Store. And some fresh oranges. He bought a coat. He found a red one too small. He found a blue one just right. It had brass buttons on it.

Then he went to buy a hat. He found a purple one too silly. He found a white one just right.

He needed new shoes. He found some yellow ones too small. He found some red ones too fancy. Then he found some white ones just right.

Here he is with his new hat on, and with his new shoes on, and with his new coat on, with his shiny brass buttons. (He has a can of polish and a cloth to keep them shiny.)

And he has a new clean handkerchief, and a new rope, and a bushel of oranges.

And now Scuppers wants to go back to his ship. So he goes there.

And at night when the stars came out, he took one last look through his spyglass. And went down below to his little room, and he hung his new hat on the hook for the hat, and he hung his spyglass on the hook for his spyglass, and he hung his new coat on the hook for his coat, and his new handkerchief on the hook for his handkerchief, and his pants on the hook for his pants, and his new rope on the hook for his rope, and his new shoes he put under his bunk, and himself he put in his bunk.

And here he is where he wants to be—
A sailor sailing the deep green Sea.

THE FUZZY DUCKLING

BY JANE WERNER

PICTURES BY ALICE AND MARTIN PROVENSEN

EARLY one bright morning a small fuzzy duckling went for a walk.
He walked through the sunshine.
He walked through the shade.
In the long striped shadows that the cattails made he met two frisky colts.
"Hello," said the duckling.
"Will you come for a walk with me?"
But the two frisky colts would not.
So on went the little duckling, on over the hill.

There he found three spotted calves, all resting in the shade.
"Hello," said the duckling.
"Will you come for a walk with me?"
But the sleepy calves would not.
So on went the duckling.
He met four noisy turkeys and five white geese and six lively lambs with thick soft fleece.
But no one would come for a walk with the fuzzy duckling.
So on he went, all by his lone.
Poor little duckling.
He walked this way and that, but he could not find the right path.
He met seven playful puppies and eight hungry pigs.
"Won't you come for a walk with me?" asked the fuzzy duckling.
"You had better walk straight home," said the pigs.
"Don't you know it's supper time?"
"Oh," said the duckling. "Thank you."
And he turned around to start for home.
But which way was home?
Just as he began to feel quite unhappy, he heard a sound in the rushes near by and out waddled nine fuzzy ducklings with their big mother duck.
"At last," said the mother duck.
"There is our lost baby duckling."
"Get in line," called the other ducklings.
"We're going home for supper."
So the lost little duckling joined the line, and away went the ten little ducklings, home for supper.
"This is the best way to go for a walk,"
said the happy little, fuzzy little duck.

THE KITTEN who thought he was a MOUSE

BY MIRIAM NORTON

PICTURES BY GARTH WILLIAMS

THERE were five Miggses: Mother and Father Miggs and Lester and two sisters.

They had, as field mice usually do, an outdoor nest for summer in an empty lot and an indoor nest for winter in a nearby house.

They were very surprised one summer day to find a strange bundle in their nest, a small gray and black bundle of fur and ears and legs, with eyes not yet open. They knew by its mewing that the bundle must be a kitten, a lost kitten with no family and no name.

"Poor kitty," said the sisters.

"Let him stay with us," said Lester.

"But a *cat!*" said Mother Miggs.

"Why not?" said Father Miggs.

"We can bring him up to be a good mouse. He need never find out he is really a cat. You'll see—he'll be a good thing for this family."

"Let's call him Mickey," said Lester.

And that's how Mickey Miggs found his new family and a name.

After his eyes opened he began to grow up just as mice do, eating all kinds of seeds and bugs and drinking from puddles and sleeping in a cozy pile of brother and sister mice.

Father Miggs showed him his first tomcat,—at a safe distance,—and warned him to "keep away from all cats and dogs and people."

Mickey saw his first mousetrap—"The most dangerous thing of all," said Mother Miggs—when they moved to the indoor nest that fall.

He was too clumsy to steal bait from traps himself, so Lester and the sisters had to share with him what they stole.

But Mickey was useful in fooling the household cat, Hazel. He practiced up on meowing, for usually, of course, he squeaked, and became clever at what he thought was imitating a cat.

He would hide in a dark corner and then, "Meow! Meow!" he'd cry. Hazel would poke around, leaving

the pantry shelves unguarded while she looked for the other cat. That gave Lester and his sisters a chance to make a raid on the left-overs.

Poor Hazel! She knew she heard, even smelled, another cat, and sometimes saw cat's eyes shining in a corner. But no cat ever came out to meet her.

How could she know that Mickey didn't know he was a cat at all and that he feared Hazel as much as the mousiest mouse would!

And so Mickey Miggs grew, becoming a better mouse all the time and enjoying his life. He loved cheese, bacon, and cake crumbs. He got especially good at smelling out potato skins and led the sisters and Lester straight to them every time.

"A wholesome and uncatlike food," said Mother Miggs to Father Miggs approvingly. "Mickey is doing well." And Father Miggs said to Mother Miggs, "I told you so!"

Then one day, coming from a nap in the wastepaper basket, Mickey met the children of the house, Peggy and Paul.

"Ee-eeeeeek!" Mickey squeaked in terror. He dashed along the walls of the room looking for his mousehole.

"It's a kitten!" cried Peggy, as Mickey squeezed through the hole.

"But it acts like a mouse," said Paul.

The children could not understand why the kitten had been so mouselike, but they decided to try to make friends with him.

That night as Mickey came out of his hole he nearly

tripped over something lying right there in front of him. He sniffed at it. It was a dish and in the dish was something to drink.

"What is it?" asked Mickey. Lester didn't know, but timidly tried a little. "No good," he said, shaking his whiskers.

Mickey tried it, tried some more, then some more and some more and more and more—until it was all gone.

"Mmmmmmmmmm!" he said. "What wonderful stuff."

"It's probably poison and you'll get sick," said Lester disgustedly. But it wasn't poison and Mickey had a lovely feeling in his stomach from drinking it. It was milk, of course. And every night that week Mickey found a saucer of milk outside that same hole. He lapped up every drop.

"He drank it, he drank it!" cried Peggy and Paul happily each morning. They began to set out a saucerful in the daytime, too.

At first Mickey would drink the milk only when he was sure Peggy and Paul were nowhere around. Soon he grew bolder and began to trust them in the room with him.

And soon he began to let them come nearer and nearer and nearer still.

Then one day he found himself scooped up and held in Peggy's arms. He didn't feel scared. He felt fine. And he felt a queer noise rumble up his back and all through him. It was Mickey's first purr.

Peggy and Paul took Mickey to a shiny glass on the wall and held him close in front of it. Mickey, who had never seen a mirror, saw a cat staring at him there, a cat in Paul's arms where he thought *he* was. He began to cry, and his cry instead of being a squeak was a mewing wail.

Finally Mickey began to understand that he was not a mouse like Lester and his sisters, but a cat like Hazel.

He stayed with Peggy and Paul that night, trying not to be afraid of his own cat-self. He still didn't quite believe it all, however, and next morning he crept back through his old hole straight to Mother Miggs.

"Am I really a cat?" he cried.

"Yes," said Mother Miggs sadly. And she told him the whole story of how he was adopted and brought up as a mouse. "We loved you and wanted you to love us," she explained. "It was the only safe and fair way to bring you up."

After talking with Mother Miggs, Mickey decided to be a cat in all ways. He now lives with Peggy and Paul, who also love him, and who can give him lots of good milk and who aren't afraid of his purr or his meow.

Mickey can't really forget his upbringing, however. He takes an old rubber mouse of Peggy's to bed with him.

He often visits the Miggses in the indoor nest, where he nibbles cheese tidbits and squeaks about old times.

And of course he sees to it that Hazel no longer prowls in the pantry at night.

"Oh, I'm so fat and stuffed from eating so much in Hazel's pantry," Father Miggs often says happily to Mother Miggs. "I always said our Mickey would be a good thing for the family—and he is!"

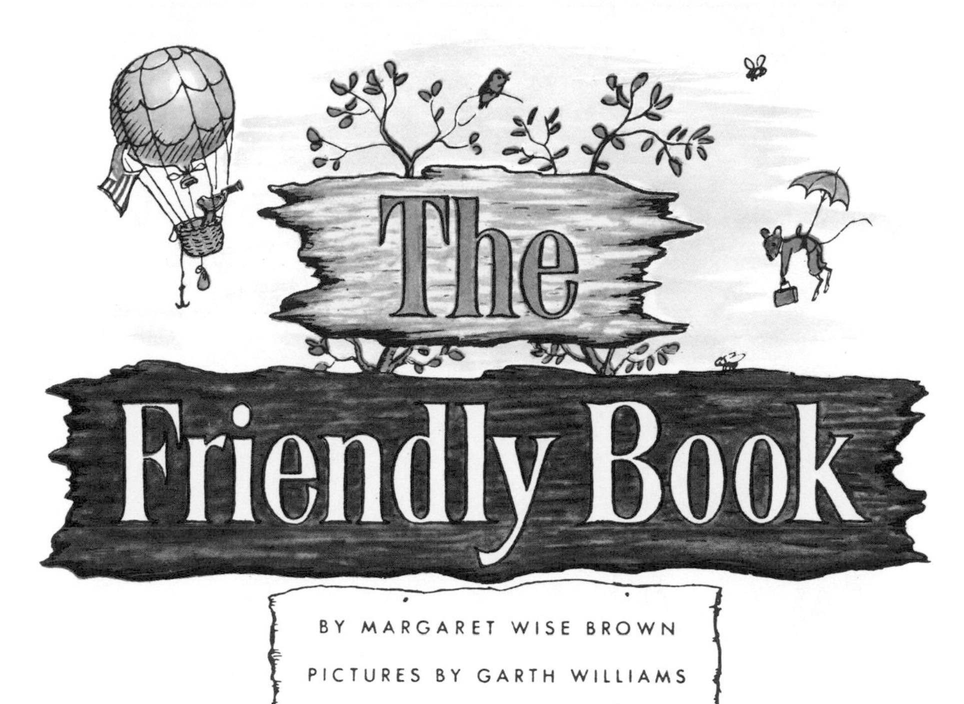

I LIKE CARS
Red cars   Green cars
Sport limousine cars
I like cars
A car in a garage
A car with a load
A car with a flat tire
A car on the road
I like cars.

I LIKE TRAINS
Express trains
Toy trains
Streamline trains
Freight trains
Old trains
Milk trains
Any kind of train
A train in the station
Trains crossing the plains
Trains in a snowstorm
Trains in the rain
I like trains.

I LIKE STARS
Yellow stars
Green stars
Red stars
Blue stars
I like stars
Far stars
Quiet stars
Bright stars
Light stars
I like stars
A star that is shooting across the dark sky
A star that is shining right straight in your eye
I like stars.

I LIKE BUGS
Black bugs   Green bugs
Bad bugs   Mean bugs
Any kind of bug
A bug in a rug
A bug in the grass
A bug on the sidewalk
A bug in a glass
I like bugs
Round bugs   Shiny bugs
Fat bugs   Buggy bugs
Big bugs   Lady bugs
I like bugs.

I LIKE FISH
Silver fish   Gold fish
Black fish   Old fish
Young fish   Fishy fish
Any kind of fish

I LIKE SNOW
Cold snow
Slow snow
White snow
Icy snow
I like snow

A fish in a pond
A fish in a stream
A fish in an ocean
A fish in a dream
I like fish.

Snow falling softly with everything still
White in the blue night, white on the sill
White on the trees on the far distant hill
With everything still
I like snow.

I LIKE SEEDS
Mustard seeds   Radish seeds
Corn seeds   Flower seeds
Any kind of seed
Seeds that are sprouting green from the ground
And seeds of the milkweed flying around
I like seeds.

I like boats
Any kind of boat
Tug boats Tow boats
Large boats Barge boats
Sail boats Whale boats
Thin boats Skin boats
Rubber boats River boats
Flat boats Cat boats
U boats New boats
Tooting boats Hooting boats
South American fruit boats
Bum boats Gun boats
Slow boats Row boats
I like boats.

I like people
Glad people
Sad people
Slow people
Mad people
Big people
Little people
I like people.

I like whistles
Wild whistles Bird whistles
Far-off heard whistles
Boat whistles Train whistles
I like whistles
The postman's whistle
The policeman's whistle
The wind that blows away the thistle
Light as the little birds whistle and sing
And the little boy whistling in the spring
The wind that whistles through the trees
And blows the boats across the seas
I like whistles.

I like dogs
Big dogs Little dogs
Fat dogs Doggy dogs
Old dogs Puppy dogs
I like dogs
A dog that is barking over the hill
A dog that is dreaming very still
A dog that is running
wherever he will
I like dogs.

MY LITTLE GOLDEN BOOK ABOUT GOD

By Jane Werner Watson · Pictures by Eloise Wilkin

GOD IS GREAT.
Look at the stars in the evening sky,
so many millions of miles away
that the light you see shining left its star
long, long years before you were born.

Yet even beyond the farthest star,
God knows the way.
Think of the snow-capped mountain peaks.
Those peaks were crumbling away with age
before the first men lived on earth.
Yet when they were raised up sharp and new
God was there, too.

Bend down to touch the smallest flower.
Watch the busy ant tugging at his load.
See the flash of jewels on the insect's back.
This tiny world your two hands could span,
like the oceans and mountains and far-off stars,
God planned.

Think of our earth, spinning in space
so that now, for a day of play and work
we face the sunlight, then we turn away—
to the still, soft darkness for rest and sleep.
This, too, is God's doing.
For GOD IS GOOD.

God gives us everything we need—
shelter from cold and wind and rain,
clothes to wear and food to eat.

God gives us flowers, the songs of birds,
the laughter of brooks, the deep song of the sea.

He sends the sunshine to make things grow,
sends in its turn the needed rain.

God makes us grow, too, with minds and eyes
to look about our wonderful world,
to see its beauty, to feel its might.

He gives us a small still voice in our hearts
to help us tell wrong from right.
God gives us hopes and wishes and dreams,
plans for our grown-up years ahead.

He gives us memories of yesterdays,
so that happy times and people we love
we can keep with us always in our hearts.
For GOD IS LOVE.

God is the love of our mother's kiss,
the warm, strong hug of our daddy's arms.

God is in all the love we feel
for playmates and family and friends.

When we're hurt or sorry or lonely or sad,
if we think of God, He is with us there.

God whispers to us in our hearts:
"Do not fear, I am here
And I love you, my dear.
Close your eyes and sleep tight
For tomorrow will be bright—
All is well, dear child.
Good night."

TOOTLE